LASS SMALL
BEWARE OF WIDOWS

D0001832

SILHOUETTE *Desire*®

™ Published by Silhouette Books New York

America's Publisher of Contemporary Romance

SILHOUETTE BOOKS
300 East 42nd St., New York, N.Y. 10017

BEWARE OF WIDOWS

Copyright © 1992 by Lass Small

All rights reserved. Except for use in any review,
the reproduction or utilization of this work in
whole or in part in any form by any electronic,
mechanical or other means, now known or
hereafter invented, including xerography,
photocopying and recording, or in any information
storage or retrieval system, is forbidden without
the permission of the publisher, Silhouette Books,
300 E. 42nd St., New York, N.Y. 10017

ISBN: 0-373-05755-5

First Silhouette Books printing December 1992

Printed in the U.S.A.

Books by Lass Small

LASS SMALL

finds living on this planet at this time a fascinating experience. People are amazing. She thinks that to be a teller of tales of people, places and things is absolutely marvelous.

To all who volunteer help without restrictions to creed or color in this Land of the Free

One

Sitting at his parents' kitchen table with his dad, Rod Brown's dark brown eyes were downcast, watching, as his fingers idly and slowly turned the teaspoon. "If she hadn't gained so much weight, I might have known sooner. But she sat there, and with the pillow behind her head she just seemed to be watching television."

Across the table on that late April morning in Temple, Ohio, Salty sat back and studied his eldest. Rod was an adopted son who was thirty-eight. His white blond hair was a surprise with his dark brows and eyes. In his raspy voice, Salty gently asked, "Are you feeling guilt?"

"No. She seemed contented. She couldn't help herself. She was just...different."

"But you did realize she was getting worse?"

Rod turned up the hand by the spoon in a touchingly poignant gesture. "It was so gradual. I was used to her not talking, not answering. With the TV on all the time, I didn't say much, and she hadn't replied to anything in a long time. She would get so engrossed with the television. It was her life."

"Did the cops give you a hard time?"

"Yeah. Pat explained the problem to them. Then they decided Pat and I had done away with Cheryl. A love-nest deal."

"How'd you handle that?"

"I was so baffled that I couldn't think. Pat scoffed. She had the doctor give a deposition. A couple of nurses and some of the neighbors testified. They were great. But it was really Pat. She's logical. No one could ask for a better neighbor."

"What's this . . . Pat like?"

Rod sighed. "You have to know that she's the one that's taken care of Cheryl for a long time. They'd both grown up in that neighborhood, and Pat had known Cheryl since she was a kid. With Pat to help her, Cheryl could stay in her own house. Pat was the only one who could convince her to get out of that chair. She got her into the shower, changed her clothes and gave her the medication." Rod slowly shook his head. "I could never make up our debt to Pat."

Probing for the kernel of whatever was troubling his son, Salty asked with a gentle rasp, "It must have been . . . unsettling for you to know Cheryl had been dead all that time."

Rod nodded. "Yeah. Pat had been in a car wreck and was knocked out. She was 'out of it' for a little while, and they took her to the hospital for tests. She'd fretted about Cheryl. There was a night nurse who knew about Pat taking care of Cheryl, so she paid attention."

"Then how come the cops got the idea—"

"There was a marked difference between Pat and what Cheryl had become." Rod put his fingers through his hair, not helping it at all.

And Salty knew his son's distress. "Are you grieving?"

"For myself? No. We had nothing left ... together. Not for a long, long time. But her life was so ... wasted." He looked up at his dad with a frown and squinted eyes.

"If she'd wanted it different, she could have changed it."

Rod looked back down at the spoon. "Maybe, at first."

"We can't judge the use one person makes of his or her life by using our own standards."

Rod replied slowly, "I know. Cheryl was a user. Pat had given her so much time."

"It was you that harbored Cheryl. You're the one that kept her safe."

"It didn't cost me much of anything. It was Pat who did the work."

"You're thirty-eight years old. You were married for eleven years. It cost you your years of making a family. It cost you time. You came home to visit twice in all those years. How many people did you have to your house or go to see? You allowed her circumstances to make you a prisoner to the house, to her routine. Now you have an opportunity to be free. And to build a life."

Rod sat looking out the windows over the landscape in back of the Brown house. The leaves were the new green of spring. And the early grasses were still lush and rich. Quietly Rod told Salty, "At the house, afterwards, it was just such a—surprise—to go inside a clean-smelling house and see her empty chair. I was used to her being there. I think it was the silence that rattled me. The television was off. I mentioned to Pat how weird it was to come into a silent house. Pat put the timer on the radio so that it was on when I came into the house one night, and it about made me jump out of my skin."

"Spooked you."

"It sure did."

Salty's rasp was gentle. "So you believe in ghosts?"

"Not if I can help it."

Salty chuffed a rasp and rose. "Come on. You've had enough coffee. Let's go out to the barn and see how much you remember about cleaning it up."

Moving sluggishly, Rod rose from his chair and followed. Rod instructed his father, "It wasn't the navy that made you this way, you're a natural-born slave driver. I was always impressed that you adopted Mike, John and me, you being a bachelor at that time. Then you married Felicia and moved here, and I realized you'd adopted us for slave labor."

Salty nodded. "Yeah. But we had the five kids to help out you three."

"No. You only spaced the kids out so that when the three of us left home, you'd still have someone to push around. And since then, you've taken in children to fill any gaps. I figure you and Felicia have raised about twenty-two take-in kids?"

"Twenty-three with Teller."

"How's Teller getting along?"

"Bob sorted him out."

After a pensive silence, Rod commented, "Bob got a good woman."

"Yep."

With some irony, Rod added, "I understand Bob had no choice. As soon as he asked to come home from Boston, after his wife divorced him and her father fired him, you and Felicia already had Jo picked out for him. Everyone in Temple knows that."

Salty nodded.

"And Cray came home from almost four years of roaming, and you and Felicia sent him down to Texas right into the trap that was Susanne."

"Yeah."

Rod turned a rather dangerous face toward his father and asked in a quiet voice, "You got a trap for me?"

Salty studied the tacky peeling paint on the sides of the house and replied, "No."

Rod looked over the vibrant renewed land and knew its restlessness. "I doubt I ever marry again."

"Just 'Beware of widows bearing casseroles.'"

Rod gave his father a dubious glance. "Now, how did you know that?"

"You forgot that I was a bachelor navy man with three young sons. We were courted. A handsome ready-made family, like that, was tempting to women. But then I met Felicia. My." He shook his head once and smiled. Then he glanced at his son. "They already started bringing you casseroles?"

"You ought to see the freezer."

"Is Pat one?"

"She's always brought us food. I had to find ways to make up for it. She wouldn't take a cent. I had her car painted anonymously. She's a gardener, and I had a load of dirt delivered. Stuff like that. It's been a real pain, trying to keep even with her."

"What's she like?" Salty asked and waited.

Indifferent, Rod replied, "She's a busy woman."

"Ahh."

Rod frowned. He elaborated, trying to remember. "A good-looking woman. I rarely see her. She'd come to Cheryl while I was at the shop. She isn't at all interested in me. Or in any man. She's not long a widow. Her husband was incapacitated for a long time. She was devoted to him and helped Cheryl almost automatically. She's just a natural-born helper."

His dad put in, "She'll either cripple you with kindness so you won't realize you need to take hold of your life, or she'll match you up with a woman you might not be entirely sure you want."

"I'm not Cheryl."

"You allowed your life to go another way and did nothing about it. You could have taken in some kids and seen to their care. You didn't need for Cheryl not to be there in order for you to change what was happening to your own life."

"You've said that before. You started saying that years ago. How could I have changed anything?"

"Had you wanted to solve it, you would have. You took the easy way out, you didn't get involved in anything but work. You did nothing to enrich your own life."

Rod stiffened. His breathing changed, his hands tightened and he shifted a pace or two. But he didn't reply.

His reaction *almost* pleased Salty. Rod still had some sand. All that he needed was a little nudging. He needed to see that he could control his own life. He'd drifted much too long.

They cleaned the barn and tidied it. It was satisfying work. Rod's muscles weren't used to such labor, but the muscle sting of physical effort was a remembered pleasure. He said, "Let's paint the house."

"Now you know that Abner isn't quite ready to tackle anything like that yet. He's still healing from that horrific fall three years ago."

"How long will you wait for him before you do something? If the painting isn't done this spring, the siding could deteriorate." And Rod gave his father a challenging look. His dad had told him to take his life and order it, what about Abner's control over the Browns?

Salty smiled. "Abner's problem is healing bones and muscles."

"For three years?"

"It was his back, mostly."

"I think he's bumming it, enjoying his control, wallowing in the attention."

Salty laughed out loud. "You could be right."

"I'll start sanding the boards and we'll see how that might stimulate Abner."

Salty grinned. Rod was responding very positively. Even Rod's brother Bob had allowed Abner to call the time. "Let me check with his doctor first."

"Okay. Do it today. I have ten days."

And Salty said, "You go ahead and cut out the dead grass under the fence there. Just pitch it over into the field so that Helen can reach it. And I'll go call Abner's doctor now."

"His . . . doctor." There was only one in a town the size of Temple.

"Yep." And Salty sauntered off.

Rod watched his dad walking away from him with such a navy strut. Rod considered that his father was built like a bulldog, big shouldered, no hips, no neck. He'd been a ring fighter in the navy long ago and had taken too many blows to his throat, so he spoke in a rasp. He was almost seventy and was a good indication that fathers live forever.

Then Rod remembered being almost six years old and sitting with the social worker, waiting. He hadn't understood exactly why they were there. He'd looked around to see if he could slip away, but the social worker had been a man and he'd just looked down at Rod and tightened his mouth.

So Rod had sat there mutinously, waiting for whatever else he would have to endure. When he'd first seen Salty, he saw the uniform. Another kind of policeman. And he'd hated Salty on sight.

Salty had never seemed to realize Rod hadn't liked him. Rod had agreed to the adoption because he figured he could get away from any man who had a job. But they'd lived on a navy base and had to be checked in and out.

Then it turned out that Salty was logical. He set the rules but he showed Rod why and how to do things, and he adopted two brothers for Rod to help raise.

For a kid six years old to be given two younger brothers had been a jolt. With the kids had come responsibility. It had been a trying, frustrating, irritating, fascinating time.

Then Salty had retired at thirty-eight and Felicia had drifted into their lives. She was a magical princess and all four males had fallen in love with her. Salty had resisted the most.

Rod smiled. Salty had probably thought he'd resisted. He claimed he had.

Rod shook his head in tolerance and looked at Helen, their cow. She'd been named after an aunt of Felicia's because she had the same big brown eyes. Aunt Helen hadn't been at all pleased to have a cow named after her.

And yet again Rod wondered how a person as pragmatic as he could have become tangled up in the Brown conglomeration of peculiar people.

Well, some of them were normal...or maybe they just appeared to be normal compared to the rest.

Rod Brown was normal.

He rubbed his face hard with both hands. A normal man would have noticed his wife was two days' dead in her chair in front of a busy television screen.

He got the hand scythe and began on last year's grasses along under the wooden rail fence.

The unridable pony came over to watch Rod work. That was all the pony was good for—as a watcher.

After a time, Rod stood up and leaned back against the fence with his arms stretched out along the top rail. He was filmed with a nice sheen of sweat. He was tired and strangely contented. He looked around and breathed the country air. It was a perfect spring day.

The sun was out, there were puffy clouds high up almost to the sky's ceiling.

He smiled. He remembered how difficult it had been for him to accept that the world was really round and the "sky" went on forever. Accepting that had released the tether on his imagination, and Salty had introduced him to science fiction.

Although Rod had done his share of behind-the-scenes work at the Temple theatre, Felicia had never managed to get him onto the stage. With her clever usage of her versatile voice, she'd tried everything. "You'd be a marvelous hero, darling. You're magnificent!"

He had no ego. She couldn't convince him. Maybe that was his problem? He had no real sense of self-worth. No matter what he did, someone else could do better.

He looked along the fence where he'd cut back the grass. It was well-done. How strange to feel this pride in having done so small a job.

He turned to Helen and said, "Have you enjoyed the grass I cut for you?"

She lifted her head and looked at him with vapid eyes. The cow's eyes held the identical expression of Cheryl's blue ones when she'd looked at Rod. No interest. No spark.

The pony came over and put his head over the top rail. Rod obediently scratched between its ears, where it itched. He told the pony, "You should have a bath and be groomed."

Rod leaned on the fence with the cow cleaning up the cut grasses and the pony turning his head to indicate the next place to scratch.

Rod thought how lucky are humans who have hands that can reach and scratch. And he was aware that he had many blessings that he'd taken for granted.

He considered all of the things he could do. All that Salty had told him and taught him. Rod thought how fortunate he'd been to have had Salty—and all the various brothers and sisters.

Not long after that, the kids came along the lane from the school bus. There were six of them. The two youngest were girls who were like butterflies. They waved to Rod and went on into the house for their after-school snack.

It was a familiar memory to Rod. This was what had happened when he'd been a child and one of many in that same house. What had ever happened to him and to his own Happily Ever After?

Rested, restless, Rod continued cutting the grasses under the fence.

Having changed their clothing to suit their chores, the six came outside already spending the pent-up energy collected in the discipline of the school day. They were noisy.

As eldest, Rod automatically parceled out chores, and the kids cheerfully separated to do those without argument or lagging. Even sixteen-year-old Saul and fifteen-year-old Ben did that. Saul had been used to supervising the others, but he had accepted Rod's directions without bristling.

That was discipline.

Rod watched the six leave him and remembered all the times that he'd directed the younger kids. Being eldest had carried responsibilities. Care.

He called Saul back. And he came readily. Rod said, "Tomorrow you should all groom the pony. He's losing his winter coat and he itches."

And Saul replied with confidence, "We do that Saturday."

"Saturday?"

"It takes all day. The damned pony thinks we want to trick him so we can ride him, and he's a real chore."

Rod laughed.

He'd laughed! How long had it been since he'd done that? He said, "You'd better be careful saying 'damn' or you'll stand up for a day or two or eat soap."

Saul grinned back over his shoulder and reminded Rod: "You're my brother."

Saul's brother. Rod hadn't felt that kinship. Saul was a son Salty and Felicia had adopted after Rod had left home, but Rod hadn't assimilated the kinship. That was odd. He watched that strong, young figure going about his business and thought: I'm twenty-two years older than he. I could be his father. And the thought sobered Rod.

At supper that night, there were so many conversations going on that Rod couldn't keep track of them all. He'd forgotten how it could be to live in a family. Everyone was so . . . busy. So animated. So alive.

His brother Bob and sister-in-law Jo were at the table, of course. They were still sleeping in the attic. Rod would have thought, by that time, they'd have moved back down to Bob's room on the second floor or over to Jo's house, but they'd sold the house and they appeared to like the attic. They'd been sleeping there ever since their wedding night, just over four months before.

Since Jo was a native of Temple, that proved the people in the entire area were all strange.

Rod contemplated the several single female guests who graced the table. Those were Felicia's contribution. Here he was, a widower for less than a month, and his mother was already waving other females to catch his eye. Her efforts were futile. He'd never again marry.

But he was kind. He allowed them to practice their flirting on him. It was something women had to do. He didn't flirt back, but he listened and he would smile kindly in a very careful manner. He knew he frustrated them. But he saw that Saul and even Ben sought the women's attention . . . also practicing.

Rod said to his father, "Why did you adopt us when you were single? Couldn't you find a woman who appealed to you? Or one who was willing?"

"Not then." Salty smiled down the table toward his unaware wife who was talking to eleven-year-old Jake.

Since that wasn't the reply Rod wanted, he asked again, "Why did you decide to adopt the first three of us?"

"I wanted a family. I was in my middle thirties. I wasn't sure I'd ever find Felicia, so I found you. And you were such a nice kid that you gave me the courage to get a couple more, so I found Mike and John."

Rod was silent. He was thinking: Salty thought I was a "nice kid" and therefore wanted more kids. Salty had never realized that at that time Rod hadn't liked his new father. "Why did you think I was . . . nice?"

"You were a good kid. If I could show you something was logical, you'd do it. If it was silly to you but

I could give you a good enough reason for it, you'd do it. I admired you."

A warm little glow lighted in Rod's chest. His father had admired him as a child. He looked at Salty. Did his father admire him now? And somberly Rod looked into his own self and didn't see anything particularly admirable.

Salty said, "I talked to the doc today. Abner has already been okayed to paint. The doc said so, and he added that Abner is milking it, just like you said. You're a good judge of people."

"Then I can start the sanding?"

"Not until tomorrow."

"Well now, Dad, I believe I can hold off until morning. You've had my nose to the grindstone all this day."

"Feels natural, doesn't it." Salty laughed and punched Rod's shoulder.

And Rod laughed.

So the next morning, wearing protective glasses, Rod was up on a scaffold and had barely started to sand the tacky boards when Abner and his son came along. Abner managed to carefully remove his broken and bent body from the car to come and stand to one side, looking up at Rod. He said in a mean, surprisingly strong voice, "What do you think you're doing?"

See? The whole town was odd. How could a man who was employable demand such concessions from those who employed him? Who was in charge? Rod looked down at the sturdy figure of Abner and replied, "You're getting fat from being so lazy."

"Lazy!" Abner was shocked and sucked in air and stomped around quite agilely, madder than a wet hen!

Rod went back to sanding.

Abner snarled, "This is my house."

"You're a Brown?"

"I get to paint this house!"

"Not from down there on the ground without a paintbrush you don't."

And Abner stormed off to the car and flung himself into the driver's seat. His son barely got into the other side and was still closing the door when the car was whipped around and roared away.

Salty came outside and laughed up at his eldest. "You're a terror."

"No. I'm an honest man."

"He'll be back with his paintbrush."

"Then he can finish the job."

Having made Rod prove he still had grit, Salty gave his approval. "By golly, Rod, you're a *man* if ever I've known one."

And the little feeble glow inside Rod's heart was a tiny bit brighter.

When the ten days were up, the house was painted. Rod had helped and was paid equally.

That grated on Abner.

Rod cautioned, "Listen, Abner, I allowed you to help. Pay attention. And you get to do the interior by yourself. I'm going back to Fort Wayne."

Sourly Abner replied, "Don't drag your heels."

And again Rod laughed. It was getting easier.

Felicia put up a good argument for Rod to stay with them. "You can work at the car lot. You can expand it. You can be in *Streetcar* this summer. Since the theater isn't air-conditioned, you can sweat deliciously like the young Brando did in the film. And you would be fantastic. You'd make all the women drool!''

"Yeah," Rod scoffed. "Thanks, but no. I need to get back."

Salty said, "I think it's best you do go back. But come see us. We need you to be around. I'm a better man after I've been around you. You're a positive influence."

Rod gave his dad a quick look to see if he was being scornful, but his dad was serious. "Positive?"

With his raspy voice, he added, "You don't know what a strong man you are. You'd take over from Bob and you'd threaten my control."

"You told me just over a week ago that I had allowed my life to stagnate."

"It was on hold. You allowed Cheryl's need for isolation to emasculate you so that you were a puppy. You're wakening. Don't you realize it?"

Rod looked around as he considered his inner self. He felt no different. He looked at his father and pushed up his lower lip while he slowly shook his head. "I'm just myself."

And Salty grinned. "You'll do."

It was the next morning, early, that Rod told them all goodbye with more of a sense of parting than he'd ever felt. He looked at Salty and said, "Take care of them."

And Salty's smile was so beatific that it was truly a blessing.

As Rod drove along the interstate, west toward Toledo, he thought about his family. The kids were a whole new bunch over whom he'd had no influence.

Think of that. And he felt very isolated, very much alone.

But he'd been alone ever since he'd left home. He'd thought that would be solved when he married Cheryl. But he'd probably been more isolated, married to her, than he had been when he was by himself.

From Toledo he took Highway 24 down toward Fort Wayne. It was a city he liked. Temple was too small and Cleveland was too big. Fort Wayne was just right.

He entered Fort Wayne on Washington Boulevard, went down through town and turned south to Rudisil and on toward the park.

His was an old neighborhood that was still cared about. They had a good neighborhood association. But Rod's house was only a place for him to stay. He had no fondness for it. It was just a habit to live there.

The house was on a corner and the detached garage faced the side street. He drove into the driveway and stopped, looking around. Why was he there?

He sighed tiredly before he got out of the car. Moving stiffly, he took his suitcase from the trunk and went to the back door of the house. It was open. How could anyone have left his door open?

He hesitated. He might walk in on a robbery? A tryst? Pat and the meter man? As far as Rod knew, Pat was the only other person who had a key. She had no reason to be in his house. Why would the door be open?

He went back to his car, put his suitcase into the trunk and closed it quietly. He removed his shoes and socks, then his jacket, and he got the handgun from his glove compartment.

He went back to the door and carefully went inside. He was intently aware of being alive. He listened. There was a strange swishing sound. It was from the kitchen.

Moving silently, breathing through his mouth, he swiveled his head, watching.

The only sound was that swishing one that came from the kitchen. He went there and stood in the door from the dining room.

It was a woman. She was on her hands and knees, scrubbing the floor. Her blond hair was up in a precarious ponytail. She was buck naked.

Two

Rod's sight of the woman was stunning. He tried to
think how long it had been since he'd seen a real live
woman stark, staring naked? She had her back to him
and was busy, busy, busy. She jiggled and wiggled and
was...so *female!*

His skin shivered and his breaths were broken. He
felt like an excited stud horse confronted by a mare in
heat. It was fortunate he had on clothing. That way,
if she should turn and look at him, she wouldn't be
startled by him. Not right away. He considered that he
should quietly leave. He rejected doing that.

He stared.

A corner of his mind did consider how busy she
was. How dedicated to cleaning that already clean
floor. It had never been dirty. Since no one had ever
really used it, there had never been any reason to scrub

it... unless someone had been cleaning it that carefully... all this time?

Had this magical, remarkable, wonderful vision been naked in his house before, then?

His hair, everything on him, was uncurled and standing out straight. He was so tight in his body that it was a wonder his skin didn't split open. His blood pounded through his veins and filled him to bursting. He trembled. As an afterthought, he lowered the gun and eased his finger from the gun's trigger.

He wondered if she was actually a cat burglar and had seen him approach. Had she stripped as he'd sat in the car wondering why he was back again in this place? Was she pretending to be the cleaning woman to throw him off guard?

Not necessarily. He'd heard of women who did the cleaning naked. There was "Dear Abby's" story about the woman in the basement who took off her clothes and added them to those in the washer. Then she put on her son's helmet because the pipe above her dripped. And the meter man came out of the back of the basement, started up the stairs to the back door and said he hoped her team won.

All that went through Rod's spinning mind, bringing his amazed attention to his own imagination, and the decision that he'd just been home to Temple, Ohio, and drunk the water that made all those citizens so strange. There was a possibility that he'd been warped by Temple water.

In spite of all those whirling thoughts, he'd never taken his eyes' avid examination from their feast. And he wondered who in the world she could be?

He didn't ask. He didn't want to disturb her. If he had spoken to her, she'd probably shriek and leap up and scramble out of the house, and be arrested for running—raw, that way—down the city street, causing car wrecks and heart attacks.

There his mind went again. The Temple water. How long did its effect take to wear off?

She was wickedly glorious. What was she doing scrubbing his floor? Why would a woman, built the way she was, have to scrub floors? She could make a lot more money just walking around, undressed that way, not doing anything... well, not right away.

He wondered if she'd liked to move in with him. If naked floor-scrubbing was a fetish with her, it wouldn't bother him.

In the slow motion of important things, he saw that she was turning more sideways. He was rooted so he couldn't counter that by moving out of the doorway. She was going to see him and shriek bloody murder. His ears flinched, waiting.

She looked up, surprised.

She said, "You're back!"

She knew who he was.

She stood up and smiled.

He smiled back, breathing like a bull about to charge.

Her eyes widened a little and she said, "Oops!" *And she opened out the unsoiled cloth she'd been using on the floor and covered her front!* Damn.

She pinkened a little but she smiled. She said, "I am sorry. I didn't expect you to come...home...yet." And she laughed, so amused.

He noted that the cloth was wet, and against her body it was transparent. She obviously didn't understand that was so. He asked, "Are you from Temple, Ohio?"

That question did surprise her. She asked, "Where is Temple, Ohio?"

"Just south of Cleveland."

She shook her head, but she didn't move. And he didn't see any reason to move, either. His view of her body was only slightly obscured and she was just really something to look upon.

With his libido urgently excited, he asked, "Who are you?" His voice was hoarse and strange to his ears.

"Don't you remember me, Mr. Brown? I'm Cindy. I live at the end of this block."

She gestured with one hand to indicate that she lived beyond his driveway. That side of the cloth slithered and he watched, riveted, but her hand returned to catch the sliding material at the crucial moment.

It took him a while to get enough oxygen into his system for his brain to recall that she'd added, "When you first came here, I walked your dog."

He was stunned. She'd been ... thirteen? But that was eleven years ago and she was now at least twenty-four. She was old enough. He felt like a salivating lecher. He felt like one foot was on ice and the other poised above a snake. Awkward. His voice thickened, he asked, "Why are you scrubbing the floor?"

"All the neighbors have pitched in to tidy up so you would come back to a clean house."

"All the neighbors?"

"Yeah," she said. "We were sorry about your wife. The cops were dumb. We wanted you to know how much we care about you. Everyone thinks you're very, very special. Me, too."

She smiled that friendly/friendly smile at him and twitched a little. He considered that she was no longer thirteen. She was a delectable woman who was grown-up. She was on the very *brink* of being a quarter of a century old. He said, "I don't know what to say."

"Shall I suggest something?"

While he became cautious, his tongue asked, "What?"

"Welllll... You could offer me a shower." She did an innocent Bo Derek bounce and looked angelic.

He froze. She was suggesting...?

"I could put my clothes on—"

What a waste!

"—but I'm sweaty, from all that work. If you wouldn't mind, I could shower first."

Oh.

"Would it embarrass you if I showered in your bathroom while you're here?"

He said an earnest, "No."

"Okay." She gave him that big smile again. "I have to turn around. Close your eyes and don't peek."

"No." That was honest. He was using it against her turning away, but she could think it meant not peeking. He watched avidly as she turned and started out the other door. She was... wonderful.

She glanced over at him and caught his stare. She *paused,* pouted and scolded, "You naughty...!" And she went on through the door, but she laughed.

He stood petrified. He'd never known a woman could tease a man that way. Well, they did on the big screen, yeah, but in real life? She'd teased him! She wouldn't be surprised if he followed her to the bathroom, ripped off his clothes and went into the shower with her.

And he wondered if she'd locked the bathroom door.

His need to know became rampant. Still barefooted, he walked around the other way and into the hall. He could so clearly hear the shower that he was alerted. He cautiously approached the door. The door was *open!*

He stood there fighting temptation. He couldn't make his body turn around so he backed away, but it was slow, hard work.

By being forthright and determined, he went back outside. At the back door, he turned with some effort and walked forward. It was one of life's little triumphs.

He went to his car and locked the gun back in the glove compartment. He then put on his socks and shoes with some melancholy. But he felt doing that was good for his character.

He took his suitcase out of the car trunk a second time and set it on the driveway. Then he fiddled around, opened the car's hood and looked distractedly at the engine, trying to spend time so that she'd be dressed by the time he went back into the house.

She'd said "all the neighbors" had wanted to help him. He didn't know his neighbors. He would lift a greeting hand if someone was outside and waved first, but he didn't visit. Pat was the only one he knew, and that was only because she'd been so kind to—

"Well. So you're back."

He turned and there was Pat Ullick. She had on old jeans and a plaid cotton shirt with the sleeves rolled up. Her dark hair was pulled back into a knot on the back of her head. She wore no makeup. Her blue eyes were calm. She appeared in control. He still wasn't, not yet.

He took a deep breath and said, "Yes. I'm...back." He remembered her car wreck and inquired, "You're all right?"

"Better."

"Good."

"Is...Cindy finished?"

"I believe so. The shower was running."

As he watched, Pat smiled the faintest amused little quirk. What did that mean?

"Have you had the chance to look around inside the house? All the neighbors have pitched in and they've done the spring cleaning for you. They are really sweet. When you're ready, you might have a neighborhood beer party and thank them all."

A party? Him? He'd almost forgotten how to give or go to parties. "Yes." His agreement was the right word, but the sound was excessively tentative. "I'm indebted to you, Pat. Thank you."

"Cheryl's problem was unfortunate. She should have been in a home long ago. You were remarkably kind about her. Very tolerant."

"You did all the work."

"I felt bad for you."

Very seriously, he told her, "You have to know I had no idea she was dead. She hardly ever replied to me. She just sat there with the TV on, watching it. I never noticed one thing wrong."

"I know. It seems that she was always that way."

"It's been years, Pat. How did you have the patience to struggle with her all that time, when you had your own problems?"

She looked at him solemnly and didn't reply.

Was she chiding him? He didn't know what more to say. What could he say other than declaring the fact that he was glad the poor woman was free? That sounded so...self-centered.

With his trip back to Temple, Rod understood the reason for his own commitment. He'd grown up with caretakers. Cheryl had needed care, and he'd been trained by Salty and Felicia to give it. Cheryl had been so withdrawn, such a recluse of a woman. He'd probably crippled her.

Rod remembered Salty asking him if he felt guilt.

As Rod's mind debated, Pat stood there quietly. He looked at her. She was so serene. What was she thinking behind that mask of stillness?

She was controlling herself from flinging her body onto his and ravishing him. And she was wondering if Cindy had had her way with him? He hadn't been inside the house long enough, had he? She had seen his car turn onto the drive and she'd been riveted by the fact that Cindy was still inside his house! Cindy! My God—Cindy, of all people.

Knowing Cindy, Pat had just wondered if the poor man would escape with just rent clothing and a few scratches in awkward places. Then Pat had seen him hesitate at the unlocked door and go back to his car for the gun. With a gun, he could have survived Cindy— if he'd had the courage to use it—or the *inclination* to use it.

Pat looked aside with finely calculated and practiced indifference, then glanced back at Rod. His libido had not yet relaxed. What had Cindy done to him in just five minutes' time?

He felt awkward. He was standing, prolonging his meeting with Pat in order to give Cindy time to finish showering and dressing. He couldn't think about what she might be washing.

Pat moved a little, as if she was preparing to leave.

She would leave him there? Alone? With Cindy? He couldn't stand there forever in the driveway. He was hit by a shaft of inspiration. "Would you like to come in for a cup of coffee? The kitchen floor is sure clean."

She smiled. "Thank you. I got that done yesterday."

Uhhh—Pat had scrubbed the floor just yesterday? Why had Cindy...? He said more positively, "Come inside." He didn't want to go back in and face Cindy all by himself.

Pat raised her eyebrows a tiny bit, as if that was an intriguing innovation. She said, "Why, that would be nice."

He wondered if he had any coffee. But they went over, and he opened the door and stood aside so that Pat could go in first. And Rod was aware that he was using her, yet again. Now he was using Pat not to solve his wife's problems but to protect himself from Cindy. His conscience twinged.

"How good are you at making coffee?" Her voice was hushed and amused. "I'm particular."

"Then you'd better make it. I just boil the grounds." That wasn't true, but he was relieved of being domestic.

"How did you learn to make it that way?"

"I only drink boiled coffee when I'm camping out."

"Ahhh. The call of the wild?"

He smiled but didn't reply. He was listening for Cindy. The shower was still running.

Pat moved familiarly in his kitchen. She set out three cups. He was annoyed by that. He wanted Cindy to leave. If she stood around drinking coffee, she would feel he welcomed her there. She would stand around and outwait Pat. Obviously Cindy was already very comfortable in his house.

The shower was shut off. The silence was potent. Rod didn't breathe. She was drying herself. She was rubbing that glorious body with a towel. He watched the floor, pacing slowly, his mind down the hall.

Cindy's voice called, "Rod? I think my clothes are in the dining room. I forgot them."

Almost guiltily, Rod glanced over at Pat. She had paused and turned to look at Rod. Waiting. He took a careful breath, lifted his head and opened his mouth—

And Pat said, "I'll get them for her."

Rod didn't know how to react to being saved from carrying Cindy's clothes to her.

Efficiently, Pat went into the dining room, and Rod trailed along as far as the kitchen door. There he leaned on the doorjamb and slid his hands into his trouser pockets.

Cindy's clothing had been tossed helter-skelter, and Pat picked them up, piece by piece, to shake each one out and fold it.

Then Rod knew that his fantasy had been true and he shivered. Cindy had seen his car drive up, and she'd deliberately set up the whole situation, and having remembered to dampen the cloth, she'd even gotten down on her hands and knees to pretend to be finishing up the floor. She'd been laying a trap for him . . . with herself as the bait.

Any other man would have taken advantage of the situation. She hadn't been surprised at all by his presence. She had stood up and smiled, then tardily, she had covered her body, after first allowing him a good look at her nakedness.

How had she managed to think of dampening that cloth so that it would be transparent? She hadn't been really scrubbing the floor. What a clever mantrap she was.

He'd been celibate for so long that even a lure as blatant as Cindy had boggled him. He hadn't known how to respond. He had never been a flirt. Basically he was an innocent.

He wondered how many men she had lured so far.

By then Pat had gathered Cindy's scattered clothing and turned toward the hall when she paused.

"What took you so lo— Oh, hello, Pat."

Rod heard that Cindy's voice was perfectly easy. Pat didn't matter to her. She showed no surprise at all that someone else knew of her attempt at Rod.

Pat smiled nicely and said, "Sorry to be so long."

"No problem."

She was wrapped in a skimpy towel. How had she found one so little? He was bemused by her calculations. He saw her sly glance at him and her darling little smile. What a handful she would be for some man.

Not him? He wasn't sure. But he couldn't tear his stare from her.

She took the tiny pile of clothing from Pat and said, "I'll only be a minute. Is that coffee I smell? Great. I'll be right back."

Should he offer help with buttons? Now where had that sly thought come from? And he watched her walk away.

With calculation, she'd adjusted the towel so that the bottom curves of her swinging naked backside showed. Rod closed his eyes. He couldn't turn his head away, but he did close his eyes. Almost.

Pat's voice was droll. "I have to admire your self-discipline."

"I've only been around her two brief times, and I find myself exhausted from just watching."

"I would give twenty cents...no, maybe a little more than that to know exactly what made you come bare-footed out of the house so quickly."

"Shame on you."

And Pat laughed a breathless, so amused, quiet sound that his libido went dangerously close to over-load. Altogether, it had been one hell of a trying day. He looked over at Pat with seeing eyes. This was the first man/woman conversation they'd ever had. She had a wickedly tolerant humor.

It took a remarkably confident woman to have handled this prickly situation. Another woman would have declined his invitation for coffee, or she would have been shocked at the obviously hastily discarded clothing littering the dining room, or she would have been indignant at Cindy's display.

Pat had been none of those things. She'd been amused, and had shared the amusement with Rod. No man could deal with a woman who had such control, such tolerance. He couldn't cope with such confidence.

That made him pensive. In less than an hour, two women had been open to his approach, and he'd declined both. Was it a flaw in him? Or had he been burned out by marriage and unable to face another commitment that might again go so horrifically sour?

He had followed Pat back into the kitchen by then and he tasted the coffee.

Pat asked gently, "Is it all right?"

He glanced at her as an acquaintance and replied, "I miss the texture of the grounds."

Her eyes sparkled in appreciation of his humor.

How nasty of her to be humorous when he was rejecting her.

Cindy came into the kitchen still buttoning up her shirt. Think of the calculation, to time herself exactly, so that she didn't break stride or have to hesitate. She knew Rod would glance up at her arrival into the room. And she, hurrying, could give him a quick glance at crowded-together rounds of her jiggling cleavage . . . as she buttoned the shirt from the bottom up. What woman buttoned up a shirt that salacious way?

She appeared unknowing. How clever. She said, "Whew. The shower saved my life. I was so hot." And she looked at Rod and smiled as if they shared a secret.

His ears turned red.

Pat said, "Did you finish?"

Cindy glanced up with blushing innocent wickedness and shrugged. "Close." And she grinned widely, so amused.

Pat offered, "I'll help you finish."

"Oh, I straightened the bath after my shower. Of course, there is the towel."

Rod said, "No problem." Then he felt the need to say, "I don't know how to thank all of you for the work. The house looks great." Actually, it looked the same to him. The only difference was the silence. The television wasn't on and the house smelled fresh.

"Do consider some kind of neighborhood gathering. We would all help with it."

"Sure." Cindy beamed and wiggled a bit.

Pat went on. "People will be coming by to offer condolences and see if there's anything you need. I had the chair taken to be reupholstered."

"What material did you choose?"

Very kindly, ignoring his censuring tone, Pat explained, "There are some swatches for you to consider. I'll get them." Pat left the room.

Cindy said, "I'm just so glad you're home again. We've all missed you so much."

He considered her. How could they miss him? He'd never been around. He hadn't been neighborly. He'd worked long hours to avoid the house they called his "home." He asked, "When did I last see you?"

"You mean before today?" She jiggled.

"Yeah."

"At the funeral."

He nodded once to acknowledge her words. The funeral had been an inward turmoil. Pity for Cheryl and relief that the otherwise unsolvable situation was finished.

He looked out the window and thought how seldom he'd been in the house during the daytime. There had been the years when he had kept regular hours, nine to five, trying for an ordinary life. Then gradually he'd begun to work longer hours to avoid coming home to the relentless television.

Pat came into the kitchen with a handful of swatches. "I'll put these here on the cabinet. You can look at them or give them all back. This is the address of the people who have the chair."

Rod wondered why she'd taken that liberty, to have the chair removed from the house? She was probably a very bossy woman.

He looked back at Cindy. She was sipping the coffee and made a face. Then she reached over and put three teaspoons of sugar into the cup and stirred it. Three. The action amused him. There wasn't any way he could comment without calling attention to Pat that Cindy hadn't liked the coffee.

It was only gradually that Rod realized each woman was carefully outwaiting the departure of the other. That knowledge was sobering. What would either of them want of him? Were men that scarce? It didn't seem possible.

He looked at his watch and said, "Well, ladies, I must excuse myself."

Cindy said, "If you need anything, just let me know. I've put my phone number on your Rolodex." She smiled in that excited, shy way that looked alarmingly eager. "Cindy Toller. Remember." That last word wasn't a question, it was an assumption that he remembered which Cindy she was.

She went out the back door, and Rod wondered what she'd managed to leave in his house so that she would have the excuse to return? Then he wondered why he thought she'd do something like that.

Pat was still there.

He turned to her, and she smiled as if they shared a joke. He kept his face sober.

She asked, "Are you very tired?"

"I helped paint my parents' house."

"That was different."

He waited. She ought to take the hint and leave.

"Have you noticed the supply of casseroles in the freezer?"

As she spoke, he went and checked the freezer. The women had put their names on the dishes' coverings. "Three are widows!" He laughed. "My dad told me to beware of widows bearing casseroles."

"I am one." Her voice was cool. She continued, "You will remember to return the dishes? When you do that, you ought to give them a little something, like a six-pack or a flower or something. Do you recall that?"

She *was* a widow. He'd forgotten she was one. One of those. He nodded, not encouraging her at all.

"If you need anything, whistle."

Wasn't that from an old Bogart film? Yeah. He nodded.

She was very obviously reluctant to leave. "I took the chair out of the house because . . . it was soiled."

"I see."

"It seemed to be the thing to do, to get it out of here. I'm sorry if I appeared to take things into my own hands, not consulting you."

"That was kind of you. I hadn't noticed before I left."

"Well, you don't tend to be around very much. There are a few things we've discovered that need to be fixed. I've made a list. There's a branch that's rubbing on your roof. And there's a pane of glass broken in the garage."

"Thank you. I'll see to them."

"There's a list of those who helped, with their addresses and phone numbers. I made notes on appearances, in case you don't connect faces with the names."

"That was very thoughtful of you." He said that formally.

"Well, I'll leave you to it, then." She went to the door.

He moved more slowly, hesitating, not wanting to either crowd her out or to appear to be reluctant for her to leave. He wanted to be by himself for a while.

"Take care." She studied him, judging, weighing his mood.

"Thank you, Pat."

"You're welcome."

Then she left. She went out of the door and closed it gently.

He was alone.

Three

Each of the casseroles would have fed four hungry men. Rod surveyed them all and was aware that each of the widows had gone to some trouble for him. But what was he to do with all that food?

Then he saw that each mass had been divided in fourths. Smart. Double sheets of waxed paper separated the portions so that one or two could be removed, leaving the rest frozen. Women were smart. Thoughtful. Kind.

He was restless. While his gift supper warmed, he paced a little. He found a bottle of wine and poured himself a glass. He saw the list of helpers and read their names, noting which houses belonged to whom. He remembered that his brother Mike had memorized all the third grade kids' names from their class picture so that when he came back from the Persian

Gulf and visited them, over in Byford, Indiana, he could call them by name.

So Rod practiced which of his neighbors' names went where. He also noted that Pat had listed no identifying comments for Cindy.

The rest of the IDs made him smile. "Teeth" was one man's.

Rod read the IDs over again and again. He closed his eyes and pictured the known houses, then he thought the names and checked to see if he was right. He was a quick learner. But those descriptions made him interested to see the neighbors and match them up. Pat was a clever woman and a good neighbor.

He ate in the silence. As alone as he'd always been, he now felt that way. How strange. He'd not had any real contact with anyone, even at work, and now with the uncommon calm of Cheryl gone he felt alone.

He avoided the sitting room but went into the living room . . . and his reach to turn on the TV, hesitated. Then he deliberately turned to a cable news station.

He watched the world. He was a part of it. He didn't really feel that, but all those people to whom things were happening had mostly not chosen to be involved. Circumstances had snared them in situations or maelstroms of events. They had opinions and beliefs and were victims. They were as hapless as he. But he'd been caught in the doldrum part of that restless sea.

And he found he wanted out of it.

That was a curious thought. He wanted contention?

He turned off the TV and went to the door of the sitting room, unaware that he braced for the odor that had always assailed him. The room was fresh. Pat had cleaned. Cheryl was gone and so was her chair. It was just a room.

He avoided the shower that Cindy had used. It was too intimate to stand naked where she'd stood. And he was tired enough to go to bed.

He dreamed of Cheryl the whole night through. He watched as she appeared as he'd first known her. Her shy smile. Her slight figure. Her fragile dependence. Her curiosity aroused and her interest shared with him so tentatively.

Her clinging to him. Her modesty. Her cat. He'd forgotten that cat. Why hadn't he given her another? She hadn't wanted one. But if he had, it might have kept her...more in touch.

He saw her in the kitchen with a fairly good meal ready. He saw all the good things. He held her again and loved her, and she sighed. She smoothed her hand over his hair and smiled a little bit, then she got up to go to the bathroom. At the door she turned back and smiled again. Then she left.

Rod wakened and lay in the night. It had been real. Cheryl had just said goodbye to him. She'd been freed of herself, but she'd lingered to remind him that once they'd had a love. And having done that, she had left. She was gone. Where?

It had been so long since he'd had any communication with her that he'd thought only of her as a completely limited person whose life was too different. Too limited. To have her come to him so that he could know that she was free and that she had warm feelings for him was a comfort to Rod. He, too, was now free. Cheryl had released him so sweetly that there was no way for him to feel guilt or grief.

He lay for a long time in peace. Then he slept in healing oblivion.

He arose the next morning with a feeling of purpose. He dressed, ate and left the house with a vigorous stride.

He drove to his auto supply and repair store. With Salty running an automobile dealership and repairing used cars, it wasn't surprising that some of his children should lean to that business. They were all good mechanics.

Rod's shop sold oil, filters and tires, and they replaced brakes and mufflers and shocks. They sold parts and batteries and mufflers and tail pipes to do-it-yourselfers and to small garages and service stations. It was a satisfying business.

With Salty's tale of his brother Cray's renovation of a similar business down in San Antonio, Rod walked into the shop that morning and looked around his own place in a different way. There's such a thing as getting used to what you see and not really looking. He'd been away. However briefly, he had had a refresher course from Salty, and Rod really saw his place. He looked at everything; then he called a meeting for that afternoon.

Since he had the morning to consider the situation, he entertained the premise that if he'd allowed his domestic situation to get out of hand, it was more than likely his own fault that the shop had suffered from similar, tolerant neglect.

He was tactful. He asked opinions on what needed changing and he took the blame. "I have always considered this a team operation. Since I'm coach, you are absolved of my neglect. Let's get things organized better."

In the weeks that followed Rod hired a temporary office organizational team to get the nitty-gritty into a computer and shape up the office. Files were cleaned up, computerized, and everything was simplified. Time was spent to save time.

Tools were organized for convenience and parts reviewed to match demand. It turned into a real shop cleaning and everyone felt more efficient.

And the place was painted.

In that time, the staff met to decide on new uniforms. Representatives from a supplier were there to take their orders. What pockets would be more convenient? Where did they need tool loops? Where did they need stretch room? Did they want grippers or buttons? What material was most comfortable? What places got the most wear—besides elbows and knees?

It was stimulating for the entire staff. They perked up and felt more professional. They were consulted and gave the questions thoughtful consideration. On some things, they had to have a couple of days while they did things so that they could consider their responses. Instead of thinking just of the repair or the investigation, they paid attention to how they moved and what they used and what tool might be better and where it should be placed.

Rod was really pleased with the staff's response. They took all the questions and suggestions seriously and they didn't quarrel about them, they discussed them.

He was proud of them all. It filled him with satisfaction to see them cooperate and solve and suggest. They were a good group.

By then, he'd finished the casseroles. After a long enough time that he shouldn't get additional ones, he'd had Sand Point Florists return the dishes filled with bouquets. He had the idea of that from the "flower" that Pat had suggested. And he'd written brief notes of thanks.

Rod was busy. In that time, he went home for his brother Cray's marriage to Susanne, who'd once lived for two years with the Browns. Salty stood in as her father. Then his brother Mike married Sara over in Byford, and Sara's long-lost father gave her to Mike in the ceremony.

So it was the latter part of June and it had been four months since Cheryl had left him. And Rod's life continued.

Cindy had almost cornered him a couple of times. On one particular time, it was in his garage.

Rod was inside, sorting out the tools to be sharpened for the summer's trimming, and suddenly she was there, a little breathless and her chest was agitated and shimmered distractingly.

"Well, hello, stranger!" She spoke so quietly that she put him off balance.

He straightened up slowly and put his hands to his back. The day before he'd helped lift a recalcitrant pump that had been a little too heavy. He'd sprung a muscle.

But Cindy was appalled. "You're hurt?"

"No, no. Just stretched a muscle too far."

"Come inside and let me give you a heat treatment."

Just the words set him off. What sort of heat had she planned to use?

He dug in his mental heels and declined. "No, thanks. That's very nice of you, but I have too much to get done."

"Oh," she said brightly. "How can I help?"

He smiled a little to ease his slowed rejection. "It's a one-man job."

"I have another one-man job I could allow you to help with."

He knew better than to ask. "I can't help you today. Why don't you ask that Fuquay guy down the block? You know him, don't you?"

"He's a zero."

"Now, Cindy, I've seen him. He's a nice-looking guy. And he handles himself very well. He had his car in and watched every minute to see how Terry handled the tools. He's smart."

"I like older men."

"Well, there's Mr. Appleton. He'd be so grateful." Mr. Appleton was all of ninety. He lived down the block, sat in his window with field glasses and claimed he was part of the Concerned Citizens' Watch.

Ignoring Rod's invitation to reject him, Cindy came to him, moving like Lauren Bacall in her first films, supremely confident, rather stiff-legged and conscious of herself. She put her arms around Rod, tilted her head up and looked him right in the eye.

Rod was incapable of releasing himself. His body had to know how she would feel against him. And his mind was filled with the naked Cindy.

She rubbed his back, put her hands up under his sweatshirt and her bare hands were on his bare flesh. And then she kissed him.

It was like searing fire licking through his body and down into his sex. He could not resist. He took control and it was he who kissed her. His hands moved and one went down to her perfect bottom and pressed her against him. He was so shocked by the impact of sensuality that his nose harshly sucked in air and he shuddered. His arms were bands of steel around her lush body and he crushed her against the front of him—that female magic squashed against the iron length of him. His muscles were stone and his hard hands dug into her softness.

She made little sounds of distress and her hands fluttered. She was startled.

He lifted his head and glared down at her. She was wide-eyed.

His voice husky and unreliable, he said, "You have some growing up to do. I'm too old for you." Mentally he smothered the fact that at the same age Salty had married a woman twenty years younger than he. Rod was only fourteen years older than Cindy.

Cindy was so big eyed and shaken by the scope of his hunger that she didn't say anything. She'd never before had a man take control from her and the strength of him had sobered her.

He released her slowly from his protesting, reluctant body. He automatically made sure she could stand up by herself, then he turned her and headed her for the door. He said, "You need to take better care of yourself."

Her nod was rather wobbly, and her steps were careful as she left his garage. And Rod faced the fact that his body was woman-hungry.

That was odd. Such hunger was a young man's. He'd been half-dead and loyal for almost eight years, starting when Cheryl had first become really strange. His body was wakening. That old familiar ache. Damn. If it wasn't one problem, it was another.

But he had the house locks changed. He knew that Cindy...and who all else...had keys to his house. Pat Ullick had one. He gave her one of the new ones. The house could catch on fire and, with a key, the firemen could get in without ruining a door.

So he stayed aloof.

He had seen Pat on occasion, but he had been very busy with the renovations at the shop and had only called back a hello or waved a hand.

With the changes at the shop completed, Rod was in his office using his new computer. He used the simple program with confidence and a rather awed feeling of competence, giving the eager computer problems and having it solve them so logically and effortlessly. It was rather heady.

One of the men came to his open door. "Rod? Can I have a minute?"

"Sure, Pedro." He swiveled his chair a bit to be welcoming and let the computer go on working. "What's the problem? Sit down?"

"Yeah." Pedro sat on the edge of the chair by Rod's desk. He was uncomfortable.

With all the cooperation, was there finally a glitch? Rod waited, giving Pedro time.

"Uhh. My wife, and the oldest boy especially, would like to see what all we've done here. I've been telling them, and they'd like to come by. Is that okay?"

"Well, sure."

"Thanks. I knew it'd be okay, but I had to ask."

"Whenever it's easiest." Rod gestured openly. "Or you could bring them by after hours. That might be safest, with the machines shut down."

"I'll do that." He grinned at Rod and stood up.

Then, as Pedro was walking out through the door, Rod said, "Wait a minute?"

Pedro looked back inquiringly.

"Come sit down a minute and advise me."

Pedro came back and sat down more confidently. "What's the problem?" And he smiled as he deliberately echoed Rod's invitation to talk.

Rod grinned to acknowledge that as he asked, "What would you think of having a staff open house here, so all the families can see where you guys work?"

"—and Angie," Pedro amended.

Rod corrected his words, adding, "—and Angie."

So that is what happened. A committee was formed to handle the refreshments. One of the younger, newer guys volunteered to bring some tapes that—he promised—were much better than those generally played. That brought blats of comments, mostly derogatory.

With Angie there, and Rod's office lady, Twila, the men's responding comments were shadings of wickedness, but not gross. One thing about having women around, the guys were challenged to clean up their chatter. Twila didn't notice their efforts, but Angie was patiently tolerant.

Rod had hired Angie because his brother's red-headed wife, Jo, was such an expert mechanic. While Angie had never been "one of the boys," she was a great mechanic. Her hands fit where a man's larger hands had to adjust or make some effort. She was quiet, efficient, aloof and a gem. And with the new power machines, she didn't have to depend on someone else's muscle to loosen or tighten anything.

Rod found that he wondered who Angie would bring to the open house. Some Casper Milquetoast? An intimidating hunk? She was the first woman he'd been curious about in a long time. She was single. Was she living with someone?

Maybe she thought of herself as male. She had chosen a masculine job, perhaps she felt masculine. He looked at that feminine woman and hoped not.

Their family open house went very well. Rod quietly told Sam, "I didn't know you would clean up so well."

Sam laughed and introduced Rod to his wife and kids.

Taking a leaf from Pat's neighborhood notes, Rod had gone through the employee files and learned the names of the spouses and their children. He did very well in remembering. And the children were pleased. They felt known.

Probably the most interesting thing to Rod was the pride of the men as they showed their families around. That was nice to see.

And he saw that Angie had brought a nice guy and her parents, and Rod noticed that Angie held the guy's hand.

With the staff open house so successful, Rod and his crew decided to hold another party for their customers and suppliers. Then they added names of those people who hadn't been around for a while and those of potential customers, such as cab companies and auto-rental places.

Along with the rest, Rod's next-door neighbor Pat Ullick was one of those who received an invitation to the customer/supplier open house.

An amazing number of people came by. The caterer had warned that was possible, and they had anticipated how many might show up. They were prepared, and the people did show up. It was very gratifying.

Rod was laughing with Angie when he looked up to see Pat watching him. When he'd finished his conversation he started in search of Pat, but he ran into a redheaded woman customer he only knew by sight. Since Twila was smart enough to insist on name tags, he saw that the redhead was Glenna Madison. He could have greeted her by name, but he said, "Well, hello, Red."

Rod knew Glenna was widowed. Her husband had been in the Persian Gulf war and had stepped on a land mine—after the war was officially over. That had shaken the whole city. Such a waste. She lived alone.

Because he had been legally tied to Cheryl and he was the man Salty and Felicia had raised, the redhead had been off-limits to him. But now he saw her from another point of view. He was free, and so was she. He looked at her differently. She was available. And so was he.

She had always managed to speak to him when she brought her car in to be serviced. She had always had something sassy to say. She flirted. Now he was ready to flirt back. They laughed, and he encouraged her to stay around until the party was over.

"I can't be too late, I have chores tomorrow." She watched for his reaction and waited for his response.

He quoted, "Live for today."

"It's been a really tough day, and I haven't had supper as yet."

"Let's go check out the buffet. We have exciting things like...ham and cheese? Spaghetti? A gourmand's delight."

"I'm on a diet."

He looked down her body and asked, "Why?"

She laughed deliciously and the roots of his body hair tickled and shivered.

He picked up a plate and served her with charming ineptness. He filled her plate.

She protested, "I'm not a stevedore." Her eyes were amused and she bit at her smile.

"I'll help," he replied and knew that he was flirting.

And Pat saw that.

He didn't take Glenna to his house that night. She had her own car. But Rod followed her home and saw to it that she got safely inside her house in her secure suburban neighborhood.

He kissed her good-night. She matched Cindy for flammable kisses, or maybe he was just susceptible?

He had to walk carefully as he returned to his car. And he drove to his house, plotting his seduction of Glenna. How soon?

The neighborhood bouquets in the returned casseroles had been so appreciated that he sent Glenna a bouquet at her office.

She called him and she was mush. It had been a long time since he'd courted a woman, so he didn't try to go to her that night. He went by the old rules, in spite of his impatient body's hunger.

There was something to be said for restraint. They were both riveted. She saw him and melted. She indicated that she was ready. He refrained, but he didn't make it easy for her.

And at that point, he had her help him with his neighborhood party. The neighbors came, and Glenna was there.

The pair was circumspect. Rod thought no one noticed. He'd catch her glance and smile. She would blush. She smiled. Her blue eyes sparkled. Her glances sought Rod.

No one was fooled.

Just the fact that he had Glenna there as Star Guest at a neighborhood party was close to being an announcement. He wasn't very smart, after all, but his mind wasn't paying attention.

He liked the teasing. His body was intense and it had been too long since he'd felt that way. It was exciting.

He knew that night was the night.

Their host's distraction was an added spice to the neighbors. And it had pleased them that Rod knew them on sight.

Rod had done an excellent job of memorizing Pat's list, and he instantly matched names to characteristics from her thumbnail descriptions. Pat had a clever and droll mind. As Rod had introduced each neighbor to Glenna, those introductions had also included Pat.

He told Pat, "I recognized George 'the Teeth' right off."

Her face stayed serious. "Did you notice he's in braces? They are almost invisible, but orthodontists are very skilled. His teeth will still be big and strong, but they'll fit better in his mouth." Pat had arranged the financing so that George, a fledgling lawyer with two small children, thought his free dental help was for the orthodontist's practice and experimentation.

It was still early when Rod missed Pat. When had she left? She hadn't said good-night. Why had she left so soon?

But Glenna was there, sparkling and shimmering in the sight of his hooded, intense eyes. She was a flame and she was scorching him.

Seemingly it took an endless time for the friendly neighbors to leave. He and Glenna made short work of the cleanup, but it seemed forever before she said a satisfied, "There. It's done."

He said, "Not quite."

She looked at Rod and smiled a little. "What else is there?"

He replied, "Me."

She laughed the most nerve-stimulating way he'd ever heard. His breath changed and he said, "Come to me." And he reached out a hand.

She didn't hesitate.

He put out the lights in the kitchen and tugged her back toward his bedroom. She didn't need any encouragement, but followed willingly.

In his bedroom, he turned and kissed her, holding her with steely arms and crafty hands against his hard chest and thighs. Then he pulled her bottom to him and his need was obvious against her lower stomach.

Their mouths clung together and parted to gasp and their bodies strained. Their kisses were deep, and hot, as he began to undress her.

He had pulled his shirt free of his trousers and opened it. He had her dress and slip down around her waist and their bodies were glued in a passionate, very serious embrace with their mouths opened and melded. Their minds were swamped by passion and they were a little out of touch with the world, they were so concentrated on their bodies' reactions and needs.

She moaned in her throat and the sound drove him crazy. He had to lift his mouth to get enough air and she said in a wavering little whisper, "Oh, Sidney, it's been so long."

Sidney?

Rod went still. Sidney? That wasn't even close to "Rod," and he drew back a little.

She was in the throes of need. Her arousal was complete. She was very ready. And he cooled.

He realized this...Sidney must be her late husband. She was using another man to recapture the essence of a dead man. She was using...him.

He took her shoulders and moved her back a little so that he could look into her face. She needed a man.

He was a man. He could give her what she needed. It was called "Comforting the Widow." Men did that. They volunteered. They used such lonely women under the guise of comforting them.

Rod found that he couldn't. If he made love to a woman, it wouldn't be as a substitute for another man.

He hugged her differently then. "Sidney was your husband?"

And she realized what she'd done. What she'd said. "Oh, Rod, I'm sorry."

"Shh. It's okay." But he continued, cooled. Holding her sweet body, he held her for comfort, not passion.

"Please."

"Ah, Glenna. You must have loved him very much. You're still grieving. You need to wait a while. You ought not use yourself this way. It's just hunger. When you've healed, you would be embarrassed."

And she began to cool. "You're very old-fashioned."

"Probably. I was raised that way."

"What difference does it make? I'm a widow, and you're a widower. We can comfort each other. I want you."

"When I make love to a woman, I don't want to be a substitute."

"It was a tongue slip."

"He must have been some man, for you to still want him so much."

She began to pull her clothing back into place. "He was."

"If I recall, the war was over. He got out of his jeep to help someone?"

As she readjusted her clothing, she turned her back to Rod. "Yes."

"It's a damned shame to lose a man that way."

"God, yes."

"Aw, Glenna, you're not through grieving."

"I miss him so. I want him back."

"There're good support groups for grieving. Try your church, and there are local groups. You should find one and get help. You're a loose cannon right now. You could turn some man upside down and not mean to do it. You're reacting wrong. You need some help."

"I thought I'd gotten it, tonight."

"You were using me. You could destroy me."

"Maybe not."

"We got together for the wrong reasons."

"What's wrong with relief? You need it, too. You must miss your wife the way I miss Sidney."

"Well, the circumstances are different. We'd had no marriage for a long time. With my freedom, I find I have the libido of a nineteen-year-old. It's body hunger. I was using you, too."

"Why not?"

"I'm not sure. I only know this isn't the way for either one of us."

"A pilgrim."

He laughed. "Probably."

They finished rearranging their clothing and moved into the kitchen, got some milk and cookies and sat in the living room talking until almost three the next morning. She was charming. He was kind.

"I must go. You're a wonderful man."

"But I'm not Sidney."

She sighed and looked aside. "No one is."

"I guess that's the first step in healing, realizing that."

She smiled sadly. "Do you dream of your wife?"

So, she dreamed of Sidney. "That first night when I came home from visiting my family, I believe her spirit came to me. She was as she'd been when we were first married. It was a very sweet farewell."

"I can't let go of Sidney."

"Would he want that?"

"I don't know."

"You need to talk to somebody who knows how to advise you."

"Talking to you has been a help."

"I don't know the answers."

"But you listened. And, Rod, thank you for your kindness . . . tonight. Another man might have been offended, or he might have been rough, taking his wounded ego out on me."

"You're a good woman."

"Yes. Well . . . Good night."

"I'll follow you home . . . just to be sure you get there okay."

"Will I see you, again?"

"Let's give it a rest for a while."

"That's probably smart."

Four

On Saturday a subdued Pat was in her garden when Rod came home from work. He left his car and strolled toward her. She greeted him, but she had no sparkle.

Frowning at her, he asked, "Are you all right?"

"Yes."

He recalled that some months ago she'd been in a wreck. "Is your head giving you trouble?"

"No." She offered nothing further.

He felt a little awkward, but mostly he felt that for some reason she had distanced herself from him. "I got the flyer for the association's Fourth of July picnic."

She didn't react.

He watched as she went on with her digging. "Will you be going?"

"I don't know."

She was shunning him? "Have I offended you in some way?"

She looked up. "No."

But she didn't smile at him or reassure him. She just slowly went back to her digging.

He said, "Pat—"

She went on digging.

"Are you sure nothing's wrong?"

Without looking up, she said, "You did a very fine neighborhood party."

Feeling she would be open to conversation, he expanded on her words. "Well, we'd had the garage party, and the people who helped with that had done a great job. It was good practice for the neighborhood party. I hadn't been involved in entertaining since I lived at home."

"You managed very well."

He hesitated. He felt she was still withdrawn from him. He couldn't press any further. He needed some idea as to why she was being so cool. There was no humor in her. She might have PMS. Maybe she just felt off center. He said kindly, "Having the party was a good suggestion. Thank you again."

She nodded and went on digging.

He waited, but she didn't look up, nor did she offer any conversation. He couldn't just stand there, so he said, "Well, I'll see you later."

She looked up at him and said a solemn, "Goodbye."

He couldn't ever remember her parting from him with that word. It sounded so final.

So, snubbed by a good neighbor and having rejected two willing women, Rod felt isolated and pensive.

He was particularly sympathetic with his thwarted libido. He gave himself pep talks. He wasn't repulsive. He'd deliberately scared the socks off a recklessly teasing woman and he'd almost been a substitute for a dead man. That thought dragged at his feelings of self-worth.

While his work was distracting enough, each day was too similar, and he wasn't challenged very strongly. Not enough. It would be nice if there were a crisis of some sort to distract him. There was too much free time in which he could feel somewhat melancholy. He was sorry for himself.

By then it was July. For the Fourth's celebration, the neighborhood association joined with three others and reserved a part of the park for fireworks. They had to take out insurance and have a standby fire brigade.

The associations reserved the space each year and that year's organization had been going on since the last Fourth. They figured and ordered what was necessary for the food, games for the children, and of course, for the fireworks.

Rod had been reminded of the gathering by the association flyer in his door. He decided to go. He took what was required of the names in the first third of the alphabet and he knocked on Pat's closed door to see if she was going, but she didn't respond.

He walked over to the park solo, carrying his contribution to the feast and a chair to sit on. He didn't see Pat as he walked over to the park.

No one who could walk used a car. There was always the parking problem and the neighborhoods involved were all within walking distance.

In the expanded crowd, Rod was recognized by a good many customers who felt familiar with him, and his earnest practice for their shop party had helped him remember names. That was nice. And he sat with a couple of the families on his block.

Cindy spoke to him but stayed a discreet distance, behaving and not wiggling at all. He smiled kindly at her.

Even before the fireworks started, he had determined that Pat wasn't there. He wondered where she was.

In that next week he came home from work a little early in the hot July afternoon and caught Pat out in that strip of garden between their yards.

He knew then that he had always looked for her. It was the first time he'd caught her outside in some time.

He got out of his car rather tiredly and stood stretching his back and feeling disgruntled. He needed a friendly smile.

He walked over to where Pat was digging. He noticed that she didn't look up and she didn't speak first. She had to have seen him or at least she had to have heard his car. Was she angry with him? Why would she be angry?

He said, "Hi, Pat."

She glanced up and said, "Hello."

Whoever used the whole word? He frowned at her, but she coolly went back to her digging.

He inquired encouragingly, "Are you putting in or taking out?"

"Adding fertilizer."

"Ahh."

She didn't even attempt to make conversation.

He asked, "Are you okay?"

Not looking up or smiling or anything, she replied, "Fine."

"Have I done anything wrong or not done something? I didn't see you at the Fourth picnic. And you left my party early. Was the party okay? Why did you leave so early?"

She looked up at him for a while and soberly said, "I wasn't needed."

"Do you have to be needed? I deliberately didn't ask your help. You've done so much for me that I feel indebted to you. I'll never begin to be able to balance my obligations to you."

"There's no obligation at all."

He felt uncomfortable and frowned. "Have you had bad news? Is there a problem? You know you can tap me for almost anything you'd need done. My God, Pat, I'm indebted to you for the rest of my life."

"No. You owe me nothing. Cheryl was a longtime friend. I did it all for her."

"If your help was just for her, I was the one who benefited. And you have to know there wasn't any other way that Cheryl could have lived out her life as she did. Without you, she'd've had to've been institutionalized. She would have had to fit into a routine that probably wouldn't have allowed her to live her life as she did. You gave her that. I owe you. If you're in any kind of bind, I'm here. Tell me what to do."

She stopped digging and just looked, not at him, but off to one side. Then she looked down at her gloved hands. "Some things can't be solved."

He squatted down near her. "My God, Pat, name it. Between us, we can do anything. I have more money than I need. I have a strong body. I know an honest lawyer. That covers everything that could trouble you. What's wrong?"

"I'm going to put my house up for sale."

He was shocked. "Why?"

"I'm going to move to another house."

"Why?"

She hesitated for a long time.

He waited.

She said, "I..." She struggled to find words. "I'm...restless."

With some gallows humor, he responded, "I probably could rent another helpless woman to give you another challenge."

She bent her head and looked at the trowel, moving her gloved fingers on it to clear away the clinging dirt.

His voice was roughened as he said, "I know. That wasn't funny. I didn't mean to be flippant. I want to find out how to help you. What's the matter?"

He saw that she was very uncomfortable. Pat was uncomfortable? He could feel it. That confidently easy woman, whose facade was so serene, was squirming inside herself.

His voice low and earnest, he assured her, "Whatever it is that's shaking you up this way, it can be solved. Let me help. It would soothe my soul to help you. I can't tell you what it would mean to me to be able to straighten something out for you.''

She looked at him. How was she to tell him that it was he who was her problem? She could no longer live next to him, listening for his car, watching the lights in his house, knowing he'd had another woman in his house. After his neighborhood party she'd watched the lights turn out in his kitchen and the only one left on was in his back hall.

Pat had sat in her window, suffering, watching. It had been just after three before he had taken that woman out to her car, and then he'd followed her in his own. Sunk in despair, Pat had sat there until Rod had returned. And she'd watched as the lights in his house had been extinguished. He'd gone to bed to sleep. Replete.

She'd paced the rest of the night with jealousy burning in her, consuming her pride. And she was appalled by her own foolishness.

"Is it some man?"

Pat was startled from her introspective pain. "Why?"

"Well." He grinned, ruefully amused. "I can understand. Remember Glenna? I thought she was hot for me, but when I got down to some serious kissing, she called me 'Sidney.'"

Pat stared, stunned.

With no visible reaction at all from Pat, Rod explained, "That was her husband. You might remember that he was killed in the Persian Gulf? It was one of those senseless things. The war was over and he stepped on a mine."

"I remember."

"We sat and talked almost until dawn—"

They'd been *talking?*

"—think she needs to join a support group. I told her that. Do you know of any? I know you lost your husband a while back. How'd you manage?"

"I could let him go. He'd been very ill for a long time. It was a relief for him to be free. A lot like the relief you feel for Cheryl."

"I'm sorry but I can't recall, was his mental, too?"

"No. Unfortunately. He was aware for the whole time."

"I didn't mean to rake it up for you."

"You haven't. Fred was a very fine man and I felt great affection for him. He was considerably older."

"I don't believe we've ever talked about him."

She looked at Rod. They'd rarely talked at all. Then she told him a not-quite untruth: "Helping Cheryl, helped me."

"I'm glad that's so. I have felt such a guilt because I allowed you to handle so much of the burden."

"I chose to do it. Remember that."

He stood up slowly and moved his body tiredly. "I have a casserole from good neighbor Allen. Come share it with me."

She had noted his tired movements. "Would you like to swim? The Abbots have a pool. I could call them, and we could go over there for a while first. Then I'll share your casserole."

His grin was wicked. "And *you'll* tell Patty Allen how delicious her casserole was?"

Pat tilted her head, acting just a little sassy. "I'll tell her you exclaimed over it."

"Choose your words carefully. She isn't a very good cook."

"Neither am I."

He turned back toward her and looked her over in an excessively masculine evaluation. "Some women don't need to know how to cook."

Her face tinged a becoming pink and she almost smiled, but the lights again danced in her eyes.

He leaned over and put out a slow hand around the back of her head and said, "Now that's the way Pat's supposed to look."

She didn't inquire what way. She didn't dare.

He went for his swimming trunks, and she went inside to call the Abbots.

The two met, carrying towels, dressed to swim with their suits covered by shirttails. And they walked through the easement to the Abbots' house.

Merle Abbot was avid to see Pat bring Rod over to swim, but she discreetly stayed inside the house—"I'll have to let you swim alone. Watch out for each other. I'm working on the Halloween party for the fourth-grade kids. In July, it's hard to think about Halloween."

They listened and nodded. Merle left the doorway, and the two were alone. They removed their shirts and eased into the still water. It was heated just enough and perfect. They swam. They paddled and talked. They lolled in the water. It was wonderful.

When they were relaxed and contented, they left the pool and stood dripping as they dried their hair. Then they donned their shirts and called their goodbyes.

Merle had to back away from the window so that she could call her reply from farther away.

Still talking, the two walked back to Pat's, where Rod left her to change while he went home and put the casserole into the oven. He showered, changed into shorts with a knit shirt and stayed barefooted.

He went out of the house, into the garage and from the rafters retrieved a remembered round metal table. He got that down and washed it under the hose. Leaving the sun to dry it, he brought two folding chairs outside.

Pat came over in shirt and shorts. She was also barefooted. She'd noted his attire from her upstairs window and had dressed accordingly. She carried a fresh fruit salad, some hard rolls and a bottle of wine.

He took the bottle and read the label as he exclaimed, "You're the smartest woman I know."

She would have liked to have taped his careless statement and have it replay under his pillow for several nights. Then she decided that most men don't care for wise women.

She added a breath of garlic, a generous amount of parmesan and a nice sprinkling of parsley to that night's casserole. It was really quite good. The rolls were crunchy and the wine perfect. The company was marvelous. They talked.

The Italian slant to the meal made them discuss Italians they'd known and loved. That led them to other ethnic groups and how varied their foods are. They each had stories. His were humorous, hers were of how people had won out over some problem.

"It shouldn't surprise me that you're a do-gooder." He poured some more wine into her very slowly sipped glass.

The sun went down and it became cool. Rod went inside to fetch sweaters and a pair of his socks for her to wear. And they still talked. It was amazing that they'd lived next door to each other for almost eight years and they'd never before talked. They'd spoken, but they hadn't exchanged ideas or experiences. They had never become known to each other. At least, he hadn't. She felt she knew his soul.

He asked, "How are we to convince you not to move away from here?" At the last possible second, he had substituted the word "here" for "me."

"I haven't yet found a house. I'm to look at one on Friday."

"I'll go with you."

"Why... that's very kind of you."

"What time Friday?"

"At seven."

"We'll have supper afterwards, if that's convenient for you?"

"That... would be nice."

With it almost dark, they finally carried their dishes into the kitchen and put them in the dishwasher. Rod decided the leftover casserole had been out of the refrigerator too long and pitched what was left.

"Would you like some coffee?" He held up the pot.

"No, thank you."

"I have nothing for dessert."

Him. He could give her some of him. She wanted some of the "serious kisses" he'd given Glenna that had tilted Glenna's mind and made her think of her husband. How could any woman in Rod's arms think about another man?

As they stood there contemplating each other, he considered that she needed some of Cindy's genes. Why couldn't she haul him down onto the clean kitchen floor and ravish him?

She said, "This was so pleasant. Thank you."

"The swimming was a treat. Thanks for including me. And your company was especially nice. Let's do this again? How often can we swim at the Abbots' without being a nuisance?"

She turned so that she wouldn't say something really dumb like, Okay, every night? Instead she promised, "I'll ask Merle."

With her seeming withdrawal in turning away, he thought he was pressing her too quickly. Is that what this was? Was he beginning to press her? And he became thoughtful. He'd better take it easy. She wasn't Cindy or Glenna, she was Pat. He would have to be careful.

So. He was going to be careful of her? Sneak up on her? What was he up to here? Pat wasn't a man's convenience. She was something for seriousness. What was he thinking about? Was he serious? He considered that soberly.

On Friday, he went with her to see the house. The woman who showed it to them was "selling" to Rod. He finally said, "I'm not buying it."

She then talked to Pat, but she watched Rod. She asked him, "Are you in the market?"

He wasn't sure which market she meant, but he said, "No. Not me."

He eyed beams and tested walls and walked back and forth on floors and he opened and closed doors. He looked at everything.

The Realtor gave him her card and he gave her one from the shop. They parted.

As the two went out to Rod's car, he told Pat, "It's a loser. You'd have to start repairs within ten months. It's got paper over crumbling plaster. The wiring is probably bad behind the walls, and I think the pipes are lead." He opened the car door on the passenger side.

Pat slid inside as she said, "Oh."

After Rod walked around the car and sat in the driver's seat, he put the key in the ignition and said, "We'll have to look at something else."

She sent a glance over at him. Nothing of what he'd said was true. She was no dummy. The walls had been solid, the floors were level and in excellent shape. The house had been rewired two years before by a reputable company and the pipes were iron.

But he was quite casually including himself in her search. He was discouraging her from moving? This might be interesting. She said, "You're very kind."

Driving along, not looking at her, but being rather pointedly noble, he said, "It's the least I can do."

On Tuesday the Abbots had no guests, so the pair did swim again. And then on Thursday they were early enough that they could swim before the Abbots' dinner guests arrived.

They saw the second house the next Tuesday. He told Pat, "It's not located in a safe area."

"But look at the rooms!"

"It isn't safe for you to live there."

"This is an elegant neighborhood."

"It *was* one."

Then Rod took Pat downtown to the Harlequin Restaurant for a leisurely dinner. The restaurant was in an old house near the center of town and the bar was in what had been the front room. They couldn't accommodate too many guests, and reservations were needed. They waited for their table and sipped wine.

Seated, the two ate at the prescribed leisurely pace as they were served the different courses. Their discussion on food preparation was a little lopsided. Pat knew names for elegant foods. Rod was a plebeian. Or he seemed so.

Of course, they were there because he had discovered the place. He was no stranger there; the people appeared to know him and greeted him with smiles.

And that night Rod kissed Pat good-night. He was careful not to shock her. But when she went into her house, he had to go over to the park and run in order to calm himself. Then he had to explain his presence to the cops on patrol after hours.

They went swimming again on Monday. He said, "Most pools are closed on Mondays. The Abbots are liberal."

"We get to skim the water."

"How do we do that?"

"You've never taken care of a pool?"

"Nope."

"How did you learn to swim?"

"In the Cuyahoga River."

"Isn't that the river that was so polluted that it caught on fire?"

"Everybody knows that's been cleaned up for years. It wasn't polluted when I learned to swim, and of course, we were south of Cleveland, and where Temple is the river flows west before it goes north to Lake Erie."

"But a *river* that caught on fire *is* intriguing. It's contradictory. Having the fire department put out a fire in a river does catch one's attention."

"Yeah. I guess so."

She guessed, "You've had this sort of reaction before."

"How did you remember the river's name?"

"Odd things settle in my mind and keep me entertained when I can't sleep."

He looked over at her with such a wickedly speculative glance that the insides of her stomach noticed.

They washed the cement around the Abbots' pool and skimmed the water and cleaned the filter. Then they swam.

No one was home. At least, Merle said no one would be. And he tried to get Pat to skinny-dip.

"You shock me."

"It wouldn't be much different than wearing that suit. It's only another skin. You wouldn't surprise me."

"I would shock *me!*"

"You're no fun at all."

So he chased her down and kissed her mindless.

They walked home hand in hand. His good-night kiss stunned her brain cells. And he thought all the hype about randiness being limited to nineteen-year-olds was relegated to Old Wives' Tales.

The third house was a shambles. The eager Realtor was optimistic, but even Pat knew it was hopeless. She said, "I'll give you a dollar for it."

And the Realtor *considered* that!

Rod took Pat to a really raunchy dive where semi-nude women danced on tables. It was a test. He watched Pat, and was she surprised? No. Her busy glances were fascinated! She wasn't blatant, nor did she make any effort at garnering attention. She was discreet, but she was so interested! There was no shock in her, just avid curiosity!

He watched her. His expression was smug. He said, "Surprised you, didn't I?"

"How could you possibly have known that I was so curious?"

So she'd shocked him. "You're a closet sensualist."

She demurred. "Surely not."

"I've watched you in the Abbots' pool. You're probably an erotic animal and no man's safe from you."

She gave him an aloof, snubbing look and said, "You're safe."

He replied, "Well, damn."

She laughed low in her throat, and his libido quivered. She *was* erotic!

They each had a bottle of beer and drank from the bottle.

There had been approaches to garner Pat's attention, and most of them she'd never recognized because Rod had been so adroit in stopping any overture. The two declined a menu, amid the free and easy calls and rowdy comments, and left soon after the hair-lifting main attraction. He took her out of there and to another place. It was a contrast.

She looked around. "This is quite different."

"Yeah, a tad."

"Staid," she pronounced.

He grinned. He ordered for them and sat back to survey her. "Can you shimmy like that?"

She lifted her nose. "Probably."

He told her, "You're a jewel."

She narrowed her eyes and considered. "It can't be that difficult." She gave a tentative little shivering shake, concentrating on it.

He swallowed rather noisily and gasped. "I forbid you to apply for work there."

She informed him, "You have no control over me. I shan't apply...but only because I would take over the place and deny the other women work they obviously need."

He smothered his laughter. "I believe you."

"Of course."

"Since you don't need to work, how do you fill your time—now that Cheryl no longer needs you."

"There are other people. There have been all along. Cheryl's requirements only took a small portion of time."

And before he could even realize that he'd said it, he said, "I could use some care."

"So could I."

He blinked in surprise. "What sort do you need?"

"The usual."

"I'm equipped."

"Ahh, how typically male. To you 'care' is sex?"

He assured her, "It's something we all need."

"Not...love?"

"It's a facet." He admitted that.

"I've never known a more secure man than you. You have no problems at all."

"In bed, I don't want to be called by another man's name."

"I can understand that."

"If I made love to you, what would you call me?" His voice was husky and low, and his look was a caress.

She twiddled with her wineglass and watched her fingers. Then she smiled just a little and glanced up. "How about 'honey?' It's a generic, all-purpose label."

She hadn't been shocked by his question, nor had she declined to reply. "You're not only wicked, you're conniving."

"It's a rough world out there. One has to adjust."

"I want to see you shimmy like that blonde did tonight."

"I don't think I'm as well endowed as she, and I'd probably disappoint you."

His mouth almost began to smile. "We could test that premise."

She laughed and her eyes were full of devilment. "You're outrageous. Didn't your mother ever tell you that you shouldn't taunt and talk to a woman the way you're doing to me?"

"Felicia only told me that I wasn't to toy with women. I was supposed to be serious and pay attention. And I was supposed to say 'please' and 'thank you' and behave like a gentleman."

"You're not being gentlemanly with me. You took me to that awful place and you tried to get me to swim nude and take off my clothes and wiggle for you."

He put his head in his hands and leaned his elbows on the table.

After a minute she put one hand on his shoulder and leaned over to try to see into his face. "Rod? What's the matter?"

"You just said it all. You know! That's exactly what I'm trying to get you to do, and the very idea of you actually doing it for me has my libido climbing the wall."

"That isn't at all true. You're just having a delayed reaction to that blonde."

"And you were avid, looking around that 'awful place' when you *could* have refused to go inside. And you could have been indignant and shocked, but no, you looked around eagerly and *watched* as if you were memorizing what they did. And you're going to go home to try it out in your bathroom mirror with the door locked."

She laughed in smothered hilarity, her hands to her face. When she could control the spontaneous giggles, she asked, "How many sisters do you have?"

He slowly lifted his head from his hands and gave her a put-upon look. "At least fifty."

"You could not possibly."

"No, you're right. But, you see, when my parents married, my dad already had three adopted sons. I was one. Then they had five of their own and they adopted kids and took in stressed kids and troubled kids, and our house bulged with too many kids my entire at-home life."

"That sounds wonderful."

"How old are you, Pat?"

"Gentlemen ask ladies that?"

"Of course."

"Oh, well, last count I was twenty-nine."

"I'm thirty-eight."

"Yes."

"You already knew that?"

"I must have guessed or been told. Perhaps Cheryl told me, when she was still talking."

"I'd like a family."

"I can see doing that."

"Having and adopting? I make enough."

She chided, "You're hurrying this conversation along rather too rapidly."

He lowered his eyelashes and almost smiled as, in a smug voice, he chided, "I only meant to ask if I'm too old at thirty-eight."

She blushed. "No."

He said with great candor, "That was all I meant. I just needed your opinion."

"Oh." She considered that after his strange marriage to Cheryl, perhaps he wanted no other marriage.

Five

As the days of July passed into August lazily and leisurely, Rod looked on Pat more and more posses-
sively. She was perfect. But she also seemed aloof.
Although she kissed with mind-blowing abandon, she
seemed not to want anything but a friendly/friendly
friendship. She teased, she laughed in such a smoky
manner and her humor was tolerant.

He could see no other woman.

He began to save things to tell her.

And she was always curious and listened intently.
She had good comments. And she bragged on him.

He felt . . . almost contented.

They swam in the Abbots' pool, always just the two
of them. Rod mentioned to Pat, ''They never seem to
use their pool much.''

"They use it every day, but at a different time," she explained. She and Merle had had a very open discussion.

They went to see films, they had dinner and they swam at the Abbots'. He kissed her good-night. He waited in fevered anticipation for them to part so that he could kiss her. It was a tear, wanting to be with her and wanting her good-night kiss.

They probably inspected every single empty house in all of the Fort Wayne area during the month of August. Not one was suitable for Pat. Rod said so. He paced and measured and looked and felt walls and studied plumb lines and not one of the houses met even the most basic standards of Rod Brown.

But he wouldn't allow her to go searching on her own. Just for her ego's sake, she would suggest that. Then she would give all her attention to the reasons he'd contrive to explain why it was necessary for him to accompany her.

He told Pat, "They take advantage of a woman alone." He deliberately disparaged male conduct to lone female buyers. But the females in that business didn't escape. He warned her, "They'll tell you one thing, and you'll find out that it isn't in writing on the contract."

He was relentlessly with her at every potential house. She would sigh. "I don't understand how so many houses are so poorly built. It's just a good thing I have you along. I would never have noticed how dangerous that tree could become in another fifty years."

She looked to see if he would share the humor of that, but he only nodded soberly. He was just relieved that he'd thought of that young tree growing much bigger and becoming a threat.

Then he would take her some new place to have dinner. And they'd return to his driveway. He'd walk her over to her house, and he would finally get to really kiss her.

That's what he waited for. Her kisses. Her soft breasts were squashed against the bottom of his ribs, his sex dug into the lower part of her stomach. He no longer allowed her to tilt her hips back from him. He wanted her to know how much he wanted her.

She didn't need the feel of his frustration to know his problem. She had her own problems. She sighed and dreamed of him. She was restless in her sleep and her body punished her.

She had become very certain that he wasn't a man who would allow a woman to take the lead. That had been clear with Cindy and with Glenna. Pat had to deal with him so that he felt in control. The basic indication of that was his marriage to Cheryl. Pat had known Cheryl all her life. Anyone could lead Cheryl. It had been that trait that had lured the caretaker in Rod.

Therefore, she decided, he needed to feel that it would be his idea to take care of her. And she would see to it that in his care of her he would find the greatest pleasures he'd have in his life.

But she realized that Rod wasn't yet ready for permanence. He'd gone through eleven years of marriage and the last eight had been a vast, trackless, lonely desert for him. He was cautious. Pat did seem to be strong and sound. Was she?

Rod knew she took pleasure in their companionship. She liked being kissed by him. What would it be like to be married to her? But his mind shied away from commitment. Cheryl had seemed all right when they'd married. Would that happen with Pat?

He looked at other marriages and he found that many weren't ideal. The partners had adjusted their hopes and made do. But most couples, even then, seemed contented.

He looked at other women, comparing them to Pat. None made it anywhere near to her status as a female. Her humor, her compassion, her interests were all quite unique.

Then he began to find little doubts. Was he good enough for her? That was a strange thought. When had he ever considered that he wasn't basically the best?

When he'd been unable to solve Cheryl, he'd wondered why he couldn't do the logical thing. As Salty had said, Rod had allowed Cheryl to control him and his life. And Rod did admit that.

But Pat wasn't Cheryl. He had never had this companionship with Cheryl. Being with Pat was a gift of time.

What would it be like to sleep with her, to make love, to lie together afterwards in peace?

His body craved to be against hers, to feel the difference of her, and it was sweet torture to hold her. His kisses were hungry, and she made him steam. He shivered and sweat and his libido groaned in frustration.

Then he began to kiss her hello, and he allowed his hands to move, brushing, touching.

He about drove her mad. What could she do? How had that redheaded witch gotten Rod to take her into his bedroom?

At the end of August, on a Friday evening, Rod and Pat had been swimming at the Abbots'. They walked home in the twilight of the summer night, listening to the crickets close by and to the migrating birds flying high up in the darkening sky. Pat tripped. Her foot caught on a root of one of the big old trees along the easement and her ankle turned wrong.

Rod caught her and he frowned at her ankle. "Are you all right?"

"I'm okay." Typically, being Pat, she dismissed any problem. But she faltered and said a small, surprised, "Ouch!"

Without asking, Rod lifted her into his arms and carried her. He was in good shape from all that swimming and he didn't even pant. He enjoyed carrying her. He looked down at her and felt powerful. "Does it hurt badly?"

"No. Just a twinge."

"I'll take you over to Lutheran emergency."

"No, silly. It's all right."

"You're easy to carry. Are you hollow?"

"No. I'm thinking 'light.' "

"Think 'heavy' and let me see if I can handle you."

She squinched up her face.

He faltered, gasping.

She was indignant, but she laughed. "You ham bone!"

It occurred to him that he couldn't remember ever teasing with anyone but Pat. And he looked at her differently. It was Pat and her sassiness that invited his response.

The streetlights had come on dimly in the late evening. He stopped under one and stood holding her, just looking at her.

She guessed, "You've lost your way?"

"My lust for you is still only in my heart."

"Uh-oh."

He smiled a little, but he still watched her. "I want you."

She became very serious. He didn't offer love. He offered "want" to her. She'd take that. But she didn't immediately agree. She watched him back.

He lifted her to him as he leaned his face down and his mouth found hers. He kissed her like a conquering hero.

She didn't struggle like a captive maiden, nor did she grab his shoulders and respond as she desired. But she did lift her mouth to meet his and she returned his stunning kiss, equally stunned.

He walked the remaining half block toward her door. He still held her as she took her key from its hidden niche, and he bent down as she reached to unlock her door. "Thank you for the ride." She shifted for the expected release.

His arms brought her back against him. "I'll take you inside."

And she wondered at his word choice, but she didn't speak. She allowed him to carry her through the door and into her back hallway.

"Which way?"

"The kitch—"

"The bath. We have to soak your ankle and I have to look at it."

With some dramatic feeling of fate, Pat rather timidly pointed down the hallway to the stairs. She was unable to say actual words because she was holding her breath.

Upstairs, as they went into the dark bath, she turned on the light.

He sat her on the closed toilet and knelt down to see her ankle. He could find no abrasion or swelling, and his probing fingers couldn't elicit any protest from her.

He looked up into her solemn eyes and he said quite seriously, "We need to soak it."

She licked her lips to make her smile behave and her eyes sparkled outrageously.

He glanced back down and rubbed his nose quite hard. "Where's some baking soda?"

"In the refrigerator." She used the baking soda to sweeten the interior of it.

"I'll fetch some."

She nodded.

But as soon as he left the bath, she stood up and skinned out of her clothing, ran into her room and brought back a silk kimono of wildly printed splashes of stark black and brown colors that were very flattering to her coloring. She had it on and was tying the sash when Rod came back into the bath.

He glanced at the discarded clothing and then at that wicked, wicked, *wicked* clinging silk and he stared.

She said, "Did you find it?"

"What?"

"The baking soda?"

He lifted his hand and stared at the familiar box.

She told him, "There's a pail in the bottom of the linen closet. That would take less water and time than the tub."

He started out into the h—

"This door." She pointed to the one between the lavatory and the toilet.

He opened the indicated door. There was a pail. He took it out and put it into the tub and ran cold water into it by rote. He carefully turned his head and looked again at that silk clinging like a thin skin to hers. He stared. He swallowed. The pail overflowed. He tilted it a little and added some of the baking soda.

She shifted to rise.

He said, "Don't walk on it."

He was sweating. His face was sheened. He was nervous. He licked his lips. He would carefully turn his head and look at her as if she might be dangerous to him.

She sat up straight and watched the pail again overflowing. She glanced up and caught him looking at her shimmering chest.

She crossed her knees so the "wounded" ankle was visible.

He stared at the water flowing from the pail while he figured out what he should do next.

She stood and he turned to her. They were only about five inches apart. He blocked her way to the filled pail of cool water. He'd forgotten it. He opened his arms, and she took the necessary step to be against him. His arms closed around her, his breaths were ragged, his body was like a wall against which her soft breasts and stomach melded.

He kissed her.

It was like no other kiss they'd shared, because they both knew instantly that embrace wouldn't end with just kissing.

They kissed to the sound of the overflowing water. Their mouths were greedy before they became gentle and coaxing.

His hands moved more surely on that insidious silken lure. The feel of her breasts under the soft, slippery cloth shivered his mind and made his body shudder.

Her senses loved his intimate exploration of her body, and she moved to make his hands' search easier for him. She made wonderful little relishing sounds that made him groan in agony.

She slid a rubbing hand down past his belt as she swallowed his exclamation.

He lifted his mouth from hers. "You wicked, wicked woman."

"What you can do, I—"

Not needing to know, he only kissed her again. Then he stepped back, leaned over as he ran a hand down her back and lifted her over one shoulder, holding the backs of her knees with one hand. He said, "Don't move. There're too many doorways and I don't want you hurt again."

"The water—"

"How can you be so prosaic at a time like this?"

And she giggled.

Still holding her, he squatted down and turned off the water, leaving the full pail sitting there in the tub.

Watching carefully that he didn't harm Pat, he turned and eased from the bath. "Which way?"

"Across the hall."

"Ahh. I've dreamed of this room."

She bit her tongue not to chatter. She didn't want to be flippant and spoil this first time. She ran her hands down his back and over his bottom.

"Just what are you doing?"

"You're doing that to me."

He did that to her. "My God, woman, you are magic."

"So are you."

"I want you."

"And I want you."

"I have to go to my house for a minute."

"For condoms?"

"Yeah."

"I have some."

And he stilled. "Why do you have them?"

"I bought them for us. I'd hoped—" And she wondered if he would feel that she'd taken control.

He said, "You did that? You went and bought some?"

What was she to say? "Yes."

"My God, Pat, why didn't you tell me that you wanted me? I've gone through hell trying to figure out if you'd be offended by me wanting you."

"We must have had our signals crossed."

He began to tear at his clothing, getting out of them.

She started to untie the sash of her kimono and he said, "No!"

She looked up, her eyes as big as saucers.

"I want to take that off of you."

She smiled.

"You're a siren."

She shook her head slowly, but she smiled and bit into her bottom lip.

"Look at you! Why haven't you acted this way before now? I've been disgruntled that you didn't have some of Cindy's genes. And you *do!*"

"When was this?"

"When I came back from my visit home."

"Are you going to tell me why you came out of your house so fast that evening when Cindy was inside?"

"You're too young." He was naked. He watched as she looked at him, and he allowed it. He stood quietly. "Do I scare you?"

"You . . . excite me."

"Do you mean I've found the one woman in all this world who wants me that much?"

"Yes. You are magnificent."

"Oh, Pat. Here, let me undo that belt."

He had a little trouble untying the sash, but she didn't help him. He finally undid it with his trembling fingers, and he slowly opened that nothing silk robe that was the essence of gossamer. "Oh, Pat, you are truly lovely." And he gasped and took breaths as if to speak, but he only looked at her.

Standing in front of her, he eased the silk from her shoulders and allowed it to float to the floor. Then that fully aroused naked man walked around her and looked at her. "The closest I've ever come to this amazing spectacle is the blonde who wiggled at that 'awful place' you dragged me to."

"I?"

"Yeah. You were trying to get me excited so I'd ravish you."

She gasped in air to protest, but he'd come around and he took her against his excited body and he kissed her as men are supposed to kiss women in that circumstance.

He made her head spin, her mouth cooperate, her hands clutch and her body go limp and excited at the same time. She felt the marvelous texture of his body with hers and the differences of them were definite and obvious.

She slithered against his hairy sheen of sexual heat as much as his hard arms would allow, but it was enough to make him gasp and tremble.

He lifted her and laid her on the bed, on top of the coverlet. She didn't object, and he didn't notice doing that.

He lay on her and kissed her as he'd dreamed. And she was all of his dreams.

Her breasts were full and swollen, while her body was soft and slithering under his. Her hands slid and encouraged, while her mouth welcomed his.

Their kisses were deep and profound...an experience. He'd never kissed another woman in that unbridled manner. It was very intimate. To him, her body was inflaming, as was her obvious willingness.

She didn't just wait for him to have sex with her. She was a part of him. That she would invite him and encourage him was shockingly erotic to him. "Oh, Pat. How I want you."

"Me, too."

"You feel ready."

"I'm about to explode."

"Wait for me."

"I will try."

He rooted down her chest and rubbed his sweaty face and prickling beard over her breasts and then took one nipple into his mouth to suckle hard and strong.

She moved and murmured, breathing through her mouth and twitching.

He popped that nipple free and paid attention to the other, his hand comforting the abandoned one, working it, kneading with the base of his palm and his widely spread fingers.

To cool their heat, he withdrew to lie beside her and she took his sex into her hand to hold it steady.

Then he lifted his head and took hold of her jaw, turning her mouth to him, opening it widely as he kissed her wickedly. His mouth was open as his tongue searched hers in a manner that showed he was not skilled or practiced. She touched his tongue with her own and felt him shiver in erotic pleasure.

That caused him to pause in the fevered play of his desire to allow their mouths to duel in that manner. That intimacy. He was enthralled. "You are driving me crazy."

"I know something that would help."

"What?"

But when she pushed him flat and began to explore him, he demurred. "Honey, we're testing me too far. I can't handle this."

"You're not handling it, I am."

He laughed helplessly.

She got off the bed and got the condoms from her dresser.

He was awkward, rolling it on. It had been too long. He made it with the third try, and she helped.

"It's been a while," he told her.

"I'm glad."

"How many men have you had?"

"There's only one I've wanted."

"Who?"

The word was very softly said... "You."

"Why the *hell* didn't you mention it?"

"I thought you'd think I was forward."

"I'll show you forward—"

And she laughed as he took her. Then she gasped. Then she moaned. Then she sighed and made relishing sounds that shivered his skin and tickled his hair roots and made his sex so hard that he felt he might hurt her. But her supine dance and her busy caressing hands, her enclosing rubbing thighs and the little smile on her lips reassured him.

He asked The Question, "Is it good?"

And she replied in a sighing hiss, "Yeesss!"

Then he had to ask, "Do you like this?" And he moved.

She countered and moved her body in a snakelike undulation.

He warned, "Careful."

"Why?"

"When I've dreamed of making love with you, you didn't move that way and you're about to set me off."

"I'll be still."

"Well, a little wiggle would be okay."

"Like... that?"

"Wow."

"How about this?" And she squeezed.

He was back to "Careful."

She went completely limp and still.

He shifted and rubbed and moved inside her.

She opened her mouth and set it on his shoulder and swirled her tongue on his salty flesh.

He rubbed his evening beard into her throat and his kisses along under her ear sounded as if he was feeding on her.

He gave her goose bumps all over her and she squeezed again, tilting her hips and spreading her knees wide.

He lifted back his head, his eyes closed as he breathed through his mouth.

She smiled. Their hair was as wet as when they had swum earlier. Their bodies were filmed with sweat as they slithered together. She gasped. "I believe now is the time to pause and smoke a cigarette."

"I thought you didn't smoke."

"I don't."

"Neither do I."

"Well, we could split an apple or a glass of wine or something."

"Why?"

"To cool down? You've been fighting so valiantly in order to persist. I thought you might want a respite."

He was up on his elbows, his face inches from hers. "I didn't know it was called a respite." He pressed hard into her. "I don't want to leave you for something like that. I want to try to prolong our lovemaking, but I don't want to go out and play some golf or swim or see a film."

"No?"

"We'll do that another time. We'll space out incompleted sessions for the whole day. Interrupting and postponing and delaying. But not now. Not this time. I can wait no longer. Brace yourself.''

She put up her arms and clung to the slats on the headboard. She spread her knees and moved her tilted hips in a swirl that his weight limited considerably. She lifted her breasts up against his chest and moved her shoulders. ''Do you notice that movement? The blonde did that at that 'awful place' you made me go inside.''

He moved a swirl inside her as he said, ''You are lascivious. I've never before understood that word until tonight.''

''Education and knowledge are important.''

''Educate me.''

''You want to know about Dick and—''

''No, I want to know about Rod and Pat.''

''Well, I can understand how you came by your name.''

''Ms. Ullick!''

''Well, you did ask.''

He pressed again. ''Tell me what you want.''

''You.''

''You got me.''

She began her supine dance, however limited by his nailing body.

With some effort, he lifted to his elbows and toes, barely from her body but giving her more room to move, and she did that exquisitely...enticing, thrilling and driving him wild.

She took him to throbbing, gasping need, but then he took over, driving into her and taking her to ecstasy as their rapture blew them past passion into erotica, to cling mindlessly on the edge of fulfillment before falling into paradise.

They lay spent and gasping for breath. Their bodies were inert. Their hands moved languidly to soothe each other because they'd completed their wondrous venture.

Without a word exchanged, with only those gentle touches to each other, they slid into exhausted sleep.

Neither dreamed.

Even though their lovemaking had taken a while, they had slept for some time when Rod wakened and found himself on Pat's bed, on top of the rumpled coverlet, with a naked Pat's head on his shoulder.

It was an opportunity not to be bypassed. He got up, rinsed himself, donned another condom and went back to the bed. He very sneakily laid Pat flat and spread her to his satisfaction. Then he took her in a marvelous, impulsive, thrilling quickness that was remarkable. It was every man's midnight dream.

As he lay lax and replete, she asked, "Are you someone I know?"

"We met at the Abbots' swimming pool."

"Oh, yes. What was your name again, honey?"

"I *knew*—"

"What an odd name! Asian?"

He pressed against her. "I'll Asian you."

"Maybe later. I've just been hit by a bus...or something."

"It was I, and I thank you for not waking up or objecting. It was a dream of mine to sneak over here and take you in just that way, so that you wouldn't notice."

"Wouldn't *notice!*" And she laughed such a delicious bubbling sound.

He eased himself from her, but lay with his face against her breasts. "Oh, did you notice that I was making love to you?"

"That was not 'making love.' That was a quickie. What we did first was making love."

"Oh. Well." He seemed to consider, then he said generously, "If you ever want a quickie, I'll give you a free one."

"Generous. Gracious. How kind."

He murmured, "Of course." And he went back to sleep.

Pat lay for a long time, a little smile on her face, her hand in his hair, playing with the strands, feeling his sleeping breath against her breast. Even asleep, his breath was hot.

Six

When the lovers wakened in the morning it was to smile at each other, and regard one another as if only now they were known.

How strange, Pat thought, were the echelons of knowing another. Their knowledge now would be different again from what it would be in another year... if they were still together.

Rod kissed her, leaning over her very similar to feeding on her. His lashes almost covered his eyes. His movements seemed lazy. He was larger than she, his length, his breadth, his bones and muscles. She felt small and fragile—but oddly protected.

She'd never had that feeling with Fred. He had been such a cerebral man. He'd been kind to her and charming, but he had never been the blatant male that Rod was. Rod even walked like a man who owned whatever portion of the globe on which he was then standing.

And she remembered the manner of his attention to her while he had filled that pail to overflowing in the tub. At the time she'd thought he felt she was dangerous to him, but in retrospect she wondered if he had been concealing from her the fact that she was his. He had chosen her. He had been careful that she not know how primitive he really was.

But his attraction to her was not simply a transfer from Cheryl to Cheryl's caretaker. A convenience.

Did he know that?

She put her hand to his head and lifted her mouth to his.

His kiss was different. He wasn't skilled. She wondered if he'd never had the practice, or if it had been so long since he'd sampled the pleasures of a woman that he'd forgotten how to do all the sensual things a man does with a woman.

He was a loyal man. He'd been celibate all those years. He'd said so and he'd been so awkward with the condoms.

The last bit of resistance in her heart melted. She felt she could love him truly now. She put her arms around his shoulders and breathed along his throat as she said, "Mmmmmmmm."

He rubbed his morning whiskers gently over her face and replied, "Yeah." He kissed her mouth gently. "I should shave."

"Your whiskers are perfect. Different enough without sanding off the surface of my skin. I like you whiskering me."

"Where?"

"There," she suggested.

And he gave attention to her neck, making her squeal and move her body.

He *loved* it. "Where else?"

Had he never done that to another woman?

She showed him the inside of her elbow. And she gasped with the pleasure of his beard's attention there.

He was thrilled and his sex was excited by her gasps and movements. So he sought and tested the places that would respond to his beard's adventuring. One thing led to another, and gradually the teasing became more intensely sexual. And again they made love.

It was exquisite. It was the stuff of dreams. It was sensual and erotic. It was leisurely and delicious. It was amazing.

They lay replete, smiling and lax. He said, "I have never known a woman could be such a pleasure. You make sex into something else. It's—" He earnestly sought the words. His frown was of concentration as he looked off unseeingly. He gave up finding the words and just looked back at Pat. "You're different."

Any woman would be different from Cheryl. Women are different from one another—as are men. Any lovemaking is different, even between the same two lovers. So his words were meaningless to Pat. They gave her no feeling that he loved her or that he considered her his. He liked her company. He liked sex with her. There were no words of love.

Being the woman she was, she didn't make plans. She didn't ask, "Which house will we use?" And she

didn't say, "You need to bring your things over here."
She didn't say those things. Fortunately.

His eyes were like those of a lazy lion whose body
was satisfied. He asked, "Would you like breakfast in
bed? If you would, go make it and I'll wait until you
need me to carry the tray up the stairs."

She grinned at him and ruffled his hair.

Then quite tenderly he told her, "I wore you out.
I'm embarrassed that I was so greedy. Would you like
me to bring your breakfast up here?"

She sassily considered that and said, "If you'll help
me down the stairs, I believe I can put together breakfast."

He frowned. "Don't you want me to give you a
shower first? I've always wanted to give a woman a
bath. Is it too soon to ask that?"

She grinned but she blushed. "Well, just a little."

"I've bathed dogs."

"Well, hey! Thanks a lot!"

He was disgusted. "Come on. You know you're no
dog. You're a really elegant woman. A gentle lady.
You scare me a little. I feel too big and clumsy around
you. I want to put my sweater down on the ground for
you to walk on." He grinned then, to make it appear
that he teased.

She laughed. "Instead, you carried me home."

His voice was low and he traced a finger along her
breast. "I wanted to hold you."

"I wanted you to do that."

"I can't want you again."

"Surely not."

"We could wait until after breakfast."

She scoffed. "That's about the third time you've mentioned food. Are you implying you're hungry?"

"Well, that just shows you're not too stupid. You can learn. You've been feeding on me and draining me this whole night long. It's time you gave me something to stoke my furnace."

She put her hand on him and said, "It's still giving heat."

"I'm working on the last of the fuel."

She started to get up as she said, "Don't expend yourself. Help is on the way."

He put his big hand to his forehead and said, "I believe I can make it downstairs all right."

"How brave."

"Yeah. Don't forget I did do this. If I faint, give me some beer."

She was appalled. "For *breakfast?*"

"For *strength!*"

"Yech!"

He sighed enduringly. "So. Now we begin to find the flaws. You don't like beer." He said that with a grim face and a tight, disgusted mouth. His adoptive mother, Felicia, would have been annoyed he could be that much a ham bone and she had never been able to get him on the stage at Temple.

"You can have *my* share of the beer," Pat countered.

He brightened remarkably. "That puts another slant on the whole situation."

While she did laugh, she thought: This is a "situation," not even an affair.

She showered alone, but when she opened the bath curtain he was there, sitting naked on the closed toilet. He said, "You don't share."

She put her hand to her head and gasped, "You must be mad! I 'shared' all night long. I need sleep!" She flung out a dramatic hand.

"Come out and I'll dry you. You should at least let me do that. In my weakened state, I won't be any threat."

She licked her grin and couldn't reply.

"You appear not to believe me."

"Do I? Why, how surprising."

He stood up and she saw that he had shaved. There was a nick on his chin. He was clean. He'd used the basement shower? Or had he gone home? Had he done that and come back to strip naked again? Greedy man.

He took her hand and urged her to step from the tub. "I get to hug you. I would have if I'd bathed you, but you're so selfish you wouldn't allow that, so I get to hug you while you're still dripping wet."

She opened her mouth to sass him but he stopped that with his own mouth and he just did as he wanted. Then he dried her carefully and took her to the bed and entered her to lie there on top of her, but he was still.

"I like being inside you."

Amused, she smiled just a little. "I doubt I can be much help at all."

"I don't intend to move right now. I'm doing as you wanted last night. We're going to take all day before we finish. We're going to join and tease and separate and wait. I'll drive you crazy so that you'll want me so bad by tonight that you'll *attack* me and ravish my poor defenseless body.''

She hugged him so that he wouldn't see the compassion in her eyes. How long had it been since he'd played with a woman? Had he ever? Had making love to Cheryl ever been anything but sweet release?

Pat's kisses then were tender. Her hands in his hair and on his shoulders were caressing.

He said foggily, ''We have to separate. If you act this way every time we get together today, I'll be a wreck by tonight. By the time you're ready to finish it, tonight, I'll already be finished.''

Her soft laughter was wicked.

He kissed her roughly, withdrew carefully and said, ''I'll help you dress.''

He picked up the kimono and held it for her. ''I like seeing you in this thing.''

''This 'thing' is pure silk.''

''I like it.'' He held the top and watched her body tu. i as her arms went into the sleeves. He watched every move she made. He saw how she was, inside the kimono, and he closed his eyes and groaned. ''Did you ever wear that—for any other man?''

''No.''

''Good. If we break up, we have to burn it. I don't think I could stand to think of you wearing that with another man.''

Quite soberly she replied, ''Yes.'' But she only meant that she couldn't imagine herself with any other man, anytime, in all the rest of her life.

That was a sobering thought. She was committed to Rod. Was she only a sexual repletion to him? And she found that didn't matter. If this relationship was only temporary, she wanted whatever he would give her.

Pat had loved Rod for years. She'd watched out of the windows for just a glimpse of him. She'd avoided conscious acknowledgment of her love until after Fred's death. Then she had faced the fact that her love for her neighbor was much more than neighborliness.

It had been her love for Rod which had made Pat care for Cheryl. The care had been carried by the twins of half guilt and half humanitarian commitment. Maybe the balance hadn't been that equal.

While Pat's thoughts had whirled through all that reality, she had completed their breakfast. Rod had helped.

They took their trays of filled dishes and glasses out onto her screened porch at the back of her house. Rod had always been aware that the porch was there, but this was the first time he'd ever been in that place. It was surrounded by trees and flowers. It was a magical place.

The August morning air was cool. The garden was bursting with summer's blooms, but there were those plants of zinnias and mums already placed so that they would still be blooming in October.

Rod knew all the work the garden required. He looked at Pat. She was so different from Cheryl.

For their breakfast they each had small, sweet summer strawberries and fresh peach slices in half of a cantaloupe. They had scrambled eggs and slices of ham. And there were fresh rolls made from dough she'd had in the refrigerator. At the last minute she'd sprinkled the rolls with brown sugar.

There were several pots of thick jam and the coffeepot was a big one. Rod sighed and contentment soaked through him. She was silent. Their conversation was easy but sparse.

They shared the newspapers, while on the tiny tabletop TV the cable news station told them what was happening everywhere.

It was Saturday. Rod called his office and said he wouldn't be in that day.

Twila questioned, "Are you sick?" Rod hadn't missed a day as long as anyone could remember.

"No. If you need me, I probably won't be available. Call Ned. He'll know what to do."

"Okay."

So Rod looked over at Pat and inquired rather belatedly, "Have you any plans for today?"

She replied, "Yes. I'm committed to some yahoo who wants to spend the day in tormenting me by intimately fooling around but not satisfying me until sometime tonight."

"Anyone I know?"

"He's sitting in your chair."

Rod leapt up and looked.

Pat put her hand to her forehead and pretended to expire.

He gave her mouth-to-mouth.

He also took her onto his lap, facing him, and showed her one phase of the tempting titillation she should expect from him during that day. He was innovative. He said in a blurred voice, "I like kimonos."

Her head back, her kneading hands on his shoulders, her breathing odd, she said, "Ummmm."

They put on casual clothing before they went to the
Children's Zoo north of town, and they strolled
around seeing all the little children feeding baby ani-
mals, feeding bold deer and handling baby chicks.

The lovers had hot dogs and ice-cream cones for
lunch. And he took her out to the car and drove her to
a secluded place, where he demonstrated how wickedly subtle a man can be with a woman.

But then she had to show how clever a woman could
be. When he was ready to go through the roof of the
car, she demurely folded her hands on her lap and
looked pure.

He was red eyed and chuffing like a bull.

She slid her eyes' naughty glance sideways at him
and gave him a cat's cream-licking smile.

He inquired in a hoarse chuff, "Do hot dogs give
you salacious thoughts?"

"No. You do."

That almost ended the day's program, right there.

August is hot and steamy in the midwest and that
weather grows corn. People don't fare as well, but Pat
knew a friend who had a natural pond. The Paynes
grinned and said, "Sure. You can swim there, if you
don't mind the fish nibbling at you." Then Paul's eyes
closed almost entirely and his smile was for Rod. "My
wife claims the fish nibbling feels like fingers."

Rod moved his tongue around his teeth and gave
Paul a grin-brimming glance.

Paul slapped Rod's shoulder. "Better take a blanket along. The water is spring-fed and likely to be cold.
But if you're active enough, you can get warm." And
he laughed again.

Jennie kept saying, "Paul!" in varying tones. And she said to Pat, "Don't pay any attention to him." But Jennie kept eyeing Rod from one end to the other with intense interest.

The lovers took their blanket and walked through the fallow field. It was filled with wildflowers and weeds. There was the path to show that the pond was a favorite of the family and their friends.

Fully aware neither of them had a suit, Pat exclaimed with excellent shock, "I don't have a suit!"

"Glory be."

"I'll feel so... naked, if you wear one. To make me comfortable, you'll have to swim bare."

"Wellll, all right. It's just humbling how much a man has to do to make a woman comfortable."

"You're complaining about having to lug along that blanket, aren't you?"

"Yeah."

"You could have left it in the car."

"If I had, you'd have wanted to be on top. Just like a woman, thinking only of her own comfort."

"Oh, can you do it that way?"

"Honey, with you, I could do it any way it took."

She laughed.

When they reached the pond, Rod saw why suits weren't needed. The pond was completely private. It was surrounded by trees, the weeds had been left alone, there were feet-beaten landing places on the banks that had been covered with pea gravel enough times so that it wasn't muddy. It was wonderful.

They slowly took off their clothes and it was immediately obvious that Paul had sprayed, for there were no mosquitoes.

Rod spread the blanket and turned to Pat. "Come here. Allow me to torment myself with you. It's only fair that I do that, so you will notice *me*. Just to see you breathe is torment enough."

She guessed, "This place makes you feel like Adam. You think I'm Eve?"

"Close enough."

"Rod, do you know how beautiful your body is? How wonderfully you're constructed. You make me want to just stare."

"You can stare another time. Come here. I want to fiddle with you."

"I have no strings."

"It's a variation of plucking. Come here. I'll let you cool off in the water almost right away. I'm so hot for you that I can't do more than kiss you."

But he did. He did a lot of things with slow movements and swirls and fingers and his mouth. Then he picked her up and with her straddling him, he walked out into the pond. For their bodies, it was like easing fire into ice.

He loved it when her puffy nipples tightened from the cold. He put his hot mouth on one and suckled, curling his body and keeping her to him, one hand on her back to brace her and the other hand on her bottom to hold her steady and not lose her.

He stood holding her, just so, and he smiled into her eyes. He slowly dunked them and came up streaming the frigid water, and he grinned at her, slowly separating from her.

He said, "I think today has been one of the most interesting and frustrating and anticipating days I've ever had in my life." Then he sobered. "You've done this with another man?" His voice was bleak.

"No. My college roommate had a husband who couldn't make love most of the time, and she would do this to attract his attention. But I've found there are a lot of couples who do this. Play at sex all day or all week."

"All *week?* I'm trying to just last this day through."

"Not all men have your...need." And realizing how awful it must have been for him to abstain for so long, she was especially tender with him. "You are a powerful lover."

"Am I? Do I please you?"

"You are...remarkable."

"Re-mark-able? Mark me again, then."

She grinned, reaching her arms up around his shoulders, wrapping her legs around his hips, and allowing him to gain access, amazed that he could in that cold water. That only proved how badly he needed her, how virile he was and how patient he was to play that day's games of temptation.

She kissed him so sweetly that he curled his hips and took over their embrace. But within minutes he straightened, released her gently, dunked under the water and rose some distance away, whooshing his head in the water.

He came back toward her and inquired with interest, "Do you notice how much warmer the water is since you got in, you hot woman?"

She scoffed and shoved a fast palm through the water to shower him. But he came to her and dunked her.

She sputtered to the surface and then tried to dunk him. How foolish. She finally climbed up his back, and he took her hands, giving her no choice, leading her to climb onto his shoulders. She was stark, staring naked and out of the water, on the chancy balance of his shoulders, and she shrieked and gasped and he just laughed.

They played one way or the other for a long time, either in the water or on the blanket. He said, "How can you look like a mermaid when most women with wet hair look like drowned rats?"

"Your eyesight is prejudiced. You still have the hope that you will get me."

"Oh, is that why I can't take my eyes off you?"

She agreed. "You don't want me to get away—yet. You think you've got a good chance of getting me into bed."

So of course he had to prove that he didn't need a bed. He even put the blanket against a tree. "See how thoughtful I am of your back?" And he pressed into her.

He put the blanket on the pebbles, to "practice," he claimed, and he drew her attention to the "give" of the pebbles as he moved on her. He sat her on his lap as he'd done a couple of times just that very day, one way or the other. He did allow her the freedom of his own body. But, again, not for very long.

"Why is it that you feel—stop that—you can do as you like with me, but when I just try to touch you, you say, 'Better not' or 'Careful' or 'Whoa!'?" She exactly duplicated his whooshing breathing of the word.

"I'm a hot man and you're a cold woman?"

She put both hands into her wet hair and observed, "How like a man to say that."

"Well, I don't hear you cautioning me to be careful or to slow down. How do you survive all my... ministrations?"

"Control."

He laughed uproariously.

She snubbed him. Sighing with forbearance. Looking off into the trees.

And he had to prove to her that she had none, and she did not.

It wasn't even very long before she moaned, "We don't *really* have to wait for dark."

"I promised."

"Then *you* wait."

"No. If I can, you can."

"You beast."

"Yeah."

His eyes were so hot and his hands scalded her. His humor was wicked, and he'd just touch her again and she'd move and beg.

Her writhings filled his shrunken ego, and her need was wonderful to him. He said, "No woman has ever wanted me the way you do. You can't know what it means to me to have you need me."

"Just a little bit. Touch me just a little."

So he did, here and there, and he touched her as she wanted, but not enough.

He lifted her into his arms and carried her back into the water.

She laid her hands on his shoulders, allowing him to hold her—which he did in a terribly lascivious manner—and she looked around. "At least *all* the water didn't steam out. There's some left." She looked into the clear air above them and into the trees. "The fog might alert the Paynes as to what you're doing with me. They'll know I've had to be cooled off a couple of times. There isn't any fog anywhere else on the farm."

"I just wonder if I will ever be able to satisfy you."

"Poor Rod." She smiled wickedly.

He sighed hugely. "A man can only try."

They lay on the blanket and napped in the speck-lings of sunlight. Their bodies were so cooled by the water that they could be warmed by the sun.

She wakened to find him watching her. And she sighed. "I know exactly what you're thinking."

And she was right.

That time she clutched him and insisted. But he would not. "Honey, I don't have any condoms with me."

"I'm in a safe period."

"You didn't say that last night."

"Well, it is true."

He didn't believe her . . . enough.

So, she thought, he didn't want to risk getting her pregnant. She wouldn't mind having his baby. She had a very sufficient income. She could do it. If she had to work for her living, with the requirements of a job, she would never flirt with being pregnant without the commitment of the man. But this was different.

However, he was adamant. "Not yet. The time's coming. Just wait a little while. It'll be worth it."

She was impatient, wiggling and trying to rub against him. "I really need you."

"Me, too."

"This was a dumb idea."

"No. I've enjoyed it. I like tasting you and playing with you and teasing you—and myself—with you. I have never done anything like this before."

"Would you kiss me?"

"I believe I have a very little one you can have."

But it wasn't, it was full-blown and sensational. And it left her gasping and restless.

He said, "Let's go back to your place."

"It's almost suppertime."

"I believe I'll get you some more hot dogs. I think those set you off."

"Don't be ridiculous. It's you who tips me over."

"Not too long, now. Come along. I'll help you dress."

He didn't help, he just got in the way. He made a remarkably teasing sexual dance out of dressing her. He was selective about which clothing went on her and which items were stuffed in his pockets.

They walked back to their car, called goodbye and thanks to the Paynes, and drove to Fort Wayne.

She said, "Drive carefully, I'd hate to be in a wreck and have to go to the hospital not-dressed this way.

"You've always worn your BVDs?"

"Naturally!"

"I'm going to teach you to live in a freer manner."

"I shudder to think what you have in mind."

"Well, now, you've had a good indication."

"If that's only an indication, I just wonder what's in store for me!"

"You'll love it."

Seven

It had been a special afternoon. The farm pond was so isolated that it was almost as though Rod and Pat had been alone in the universe. That was the cherished desire of all people who are that intensely involved. They never believe anyone else would ever be necessary.

Taking possessive glances at Pat, Rod drove them back to Fort Wayne, over to SouthGate and to Krogers. Fortunately, while it was a large store, it also served as a neighborhood grocery.

The two shoppers weren't very tidy. They looked as if they'd spent a day out-of-doors, without hats and in or on water. Their noses were sunburned and their clothes were quite rumpled.

Fort Wayne is noted for its summer exodus to cottages on the various lakes north of the city. So there were guesses from the friendly clerks. "You've been to one of the lakes."

Since farm ponds could be called minilakes, Rod and Pat only laughed and agreed.

They selected some lobster tails and shrimp for their dinner. Then they drove back to Pat's.

She told her guest, "I need a shower. I'll put the tails out to thaw. Would you like some wine?"

"I'll bring you a glass. Go ahead."

Although he'd hurried, she was already in the shower. He stripped quickly and opened the curtain.

"Rod! What are you doing?"

"I want to bathe you."

She demurred.

He protested, "But I've been naked in a pond with you all afternoon, why are you shy about letting me bathe you? It can't be modesty. There isn't anywhere on you that I haven't touched."

Men can be so unknowing. She sighed, "It's different."

"You're not."

"That again. If I'm not any different from any other woman, what's the need?"

"I like handling you."

"You've done a lot of that."

He watched her busily washing. "I could do that much easier than you can."

"If I let you wash me, you have to know what will happen."

"No, it won't. I have great control."

She laughed a delicious sound.

"You doubt me?"

"We aren't testing it."

It was his turn to sigh. "You need a room shower so that I can watch easier."

"What's so fascinating?"

"If I have to explain, you haven't the wits to grasp the premise."

"So now I'm a premise?"

He studied her. "What else have you been?"

She bit her tongue and asked vaguely, "Hmm?" But she ducked her head under the shower and couldn't hear his repeated query.

She rinsed, and he was fascinated.

And she suddenly realized he might never have seen a woman bathe—or bathed one. She took the towel from his hands as she stepped from the tub and she said, "Okay. You can do the next one."

"Good. I'll take you right outside and roll you in the dirt."

"I'm hungry."

His voice smoky, he curled his body as he reached. "So'm I."

"For *food!*"

"You're so prosaic." His voice was disgruntled.

But she laughed, left him to shower and went to her room to dress in shorts and a cotton pullover.

Their entire supper was one long tease. His advances and her counterings. She laughed so low in her throat that the hairs on his body lifted as if he'd stumbled into an electrical force field.

She said, "Taste this." And she'd feed him a bit of cracker with shining black caviar. He'd watch her as he nibbled on it . . . and sucked her fingers.

He put a shrimp between his teeth and said around it, "It's too big for me, take half."

And she smiled her cat's smile and raised up on tiptoe to battle for half. He didn't lean his head down for her to reach his mouth, so she had to slide up his body, and he put his lips around the rest of the shrimp.

So Pat not only had to stand up on her tiptoes and strain along his body to reach his mouth, but she had to struggle to open his lips. Then she had to turn her head and try to bite off her half of the shrimp against his teeth.

She stepped back, chewing and laughing.

He said, "You probably had pirates as ancestors, since you forage so handily. You took the food right out of my mouth."

"Yes." She gave him a saucy glance.

"I'm not at all surprised."

"And your ancestors?" She invited him to confess.

He didn't even hesitate. "U.S. Navy. You know how they handle pirates?"

"Uh-oh."

He crowded her so that she was against the refrigerator. "You owe a forfeit."

"I have no valuables."

"Then you'll have to think of something else I need."

"Uhhhh."

"Need some help?" He pressed himself against her.

"I need food."

"If you think I'm going to feed you shrimp and let you climb all over me to get it, you must think I'm made of iron."

She took hold of him. "Yes."

And he laughed.

She slid away and managed to get the lobster tails on a plate lined with green grape leaves from her garden fence. She added small bowls of tartar sauce. There were fresh rolls and a vegetable salad, with sherbet for dessert.

She served him on the screened porch at the back of her house. The candles were on a side table, and outside small ground lamps had been placed among the flowers. She'd contrived a special enchantment.

But he knew it wasn't the food or the lighting. It was she. And how he felt about her scared him.

She inquired, "Have you been home in the last couple of days? I wonder if your house is still there."

"I'm scared I'll find Cindy inside the house."

"Ahh. As you found her when you came home from Ohio?"

That she called his house "home" sounded strange. "Come with me so that I'll have protection?"

She guessed, "Cindy met you inside the house and offered to seduce you...out of compassion, since you were a new widower?"

That was close. He shook his head at Pat and tsked. "I would never have believed you could be so curious. Do you know how long ago that happened?"

She grinned wickedly. "What?"

And he laughed.

After they ate, he led her to his house. They entered and the silent house smelled fresh. He got the mail and shuffled through it. There was the monthly letter from Felicia and one of Salty's two-sentence notes. His adopted father had written: "How're'ya doing? We need to hear from you."

So Rod went to the phone and dialed the number in Temple, Ohio. Only the kids were there. They talked to Rod in good humor. Saul complained that there weren't any girls available in Temple, and if his big brother was any kind of a man, he would round up some and bring them to Temple . . . for him.

Rod scoffed. "If I can find any, I'll keep them for myself."

Saul replied, "That's probably best. Your idea of a woman is too old for me."

Rod looked over at Pat and replied to Saul, "Yeah." He asked that they give his love to Felicia and Salty—

"Salty?" Saul scoffed. "If I tried to do that, he'd knuckle my head. He's barely talking to me."

Rod snapped, "What have you done?"

Saul made his voice a Salty-rasp and replied, "I . . . didn't . . . clean the barn . . . well enough."

Rod remembered those days. He amended, "Then just say I'm thinking about him. That ought to be neutral enough. And tell him I had supper with a widow."

"I can handle that."

Rod talked to the other three boys and to the two little girls. He told them all good-night and he set the phone back into the cradle, conscious that Pat had listened. He looked up and saw her smile.

He tilted his head sideways. "What did I say that made you smile?"

"I don't know what it's like to talk to a family that way. I was an only child."

"Do you realize that all the kids now left at home were adopted?"

"That's what I should do. Adopt some."

"Can't you have children?"

"I've never tried."

"Well, we could practice on the mechanics of doing that."

"Now I'm a mech—" But she stopped herself.

He waited, watching her, and he narrowed his eyes. "You've said something like that a couple of times. That—uh—you're a 'premise.' What do you mean?"

She was reluctant.

He saw that she blushed a little and shifted to rise from her chair.

He said, "Let me." And he put one arm around her waist and one under her knees, then he lifted her.

He was in his own house. He carried her around, bending so that she could reach to turn off the lights, then he carried her back to his room.

Pat thought of the night that, from her own window across his driveway, she had watched the lights turned out in Rod's house. Pat had known that Glenna was with him at that time, and the agony Pat had suffered as she imagined Rod making love to that redhead had been intense.

His bed wasn't made.

His bed was seldom made up, unless the cleaning lady had just changed the sheets. He didn't notice that. He was conscious only that she was in his house and he was going to make love to her there on his bed. "You know why I brought you over here?"

Of course she did, but she replied, busily instructive, "I suggested you should check your house and your answering machine. There was the possibility that someone might have wanted to get in touch with you."

She had briefly distracted him, so he commented, "You're very thoughtful of other people."

"I've had the time. It does take time."

"You care about people."

"I haven't even a portion of something like your big family to care about me. I've had to make my own circle of people to think about."

"You can think about me. I need some attention."

"What sort?"

"Take off your clothes, and I'll explain as I go along."

She put a thoughtful finger to her forehead. "'Take off my clothes' in order to listen?" She gestured with that hand, palm up. "That's a strange way of doing things. You plan to 'go along.' Go along...what?"

"You."

"Why...how fascinating. Exactly how do you do that?"

He replied generously, "I'm willing to demonstrate."

"Do I lie down on the floor and do you walk on my back like the Japanese do?"

"You lie down—but on the bed."

"Well, that would be softer."

"Here, let me help."

She demurred. "I've taken off my clothes before now, and I can do it very easily. I have practiced."

"Be quiet. I'm being helpful."

"Oh." She dropped her hands and stood straight and still, looking interested, her eyes moving busily.

"Haven't you ever been seduced? You're being distracting."

She did not want this first time in his house to be anything like his attempt must have been with Glenna. It had probably been hot and steamy and intense. Therefore she said with great patience, "I've tried to distract you this whole day and all you've wanted to do was bathe me and do salacious things to my body."

"Well . . . yes."

"I believe you're a sensualist."

"Yeah."

"Oh. I believe that explains a lot."

"Does it explain this?" He touched her intimately and he kissed her in places that surprised her.

"I'm . . . not sure."

"How about this?" He moved aside parts of her clothing and his flesh made contact with hers.

"You're shivering my nervous system."

"Just your nerves?"

She elaborated, "—and my cells, and strange places that I've never known I had."

"Like . . . where? Here?"

"Lower."

"Here?"

"Uhh . . . uhhhh . . . lower?"

"Here?"

"Yeeeessssss."

"Well, you are a scandal! My daddy told me there would be women like you. Here, let's get the rest of this stuff out of the way so I can find out just how depraved you really are!"

"Why do you need to know that?"

And with distracted impatience, he explained, "I can't help you to reform until I know the extent of what needs to be done about you."

"Oh. I hadn't realized that."

"There's probably a whole *ton* of things I'm going to have to do, to see how far I've got to go. This could be exhausting. Do you have a couple of months free?"

"I'll check my calendar." Her voice was earnest and she looked at him with big, serious eyes.

"I'm glad you have a good attitude. It's best that you're willing for me to understand just what all I have to do in order to straighten you out."

She stood straight.

He chided, "When you do that your breasts stick out."

"Sorry." She slumped.

"Now the curve of your back is seductive."

"Oh." She stood almost straight.

"Your breasts again."

She put her hands on them to try to flatten them.

He cleared his foggy throat and said in a helpful way, "I'll do that for you."

But try as he would with rubbing and pushing and moving them around, they stayed put and stuck out.

But he also stuck out, and she licked her lips as she very seriously noted that and, also being helpful, she pushed it over to the side and held it there.

"What are you doing?"

"I thought you didn't want things to stick out."

"Uh. Well. There's a way of solving that very thing."

"How?"

"Glad you asked. It's what I intend showing you. Now this is a simple process that's easy to learn. Pay attention. We'll go over this a couple of times and I'll grade you on it."

She waggled him. "How fascinating."

"Quit that."

"Why?"

"That's not the way it's supposed to be done."

"Then . . . how?"

So he had to show her. He had to show her how to lie down and what to do. She questioned. He explained, really rather raggedly. She touched and grasped and slithered. He gasped and sweat and shivered. Then he said, in a rough and foggy voice, "Hold still."

She did for as long as she thought was necessary, but he panted and groaned, so she just went on and did all sorts of things. They thrashed around and wiggled and she squeaked and carried on remarkably, so that lesson was soon over.

Some long time later, she said amid the tangle of inert bodies there on the bed, "I wasn't paying enough attention and I'm afraid I didn't realize what all was going on or coming off, whichever."

"You mean I'll have to do all that . . . again?"

"Sorry."

"The things a man has to do in his life would boggle a Martian."

"Perhaps."

"You've met one?"

"Perhaps."

"How *would* you know?"

"The third eye."

"Where?"

"On your forehead."

"Now, when did you see that?"

"When I took off my clothes. You peeked with your third eye."

"Damn. We are warned about that very thing. You do remember that I was adopted by Salty and Felicia? I doubt they know. You should have let me take off your clothes and I wouldn't have been so shocked."

"I was the shocked one. You Martians have strange ways. But quick."

Somewhat disgruntled, he complained, "I wasn't ready."

"Oh, yes, you were."

"I was not. I wanted to go slow and steamy. But no, you have to get all excited and just take over and go wild!"

She snorted. "Well, what did you expect after you'd been flirting with me this whole day?"

"*Flirting?* What I've been doing with you today can hardly be described with a word as . . . insipid . . . as 'flirting.'"

She considered and replied, "Your tone of voice with 'insipid' was marvelously distasteful. You made it sound as if the very taste of saying the word was repugnant."

"Thank you."

"Basically, you are incapable of being insipid."

"I appreciate that observation."

"It could be a lack in you," she warned. "No sensitivity."

"Naw."

"I'll have to observe."

"Do that." Then he groaned pathetically. "Do you realize that tomorrow we will have to repeat this whole bloody day all over again? We'll have to start with sex and then tease and taunt each other for a whole 'nother day? I'm not sure I can handle another day of frustration as well as I did today."

"Good grief!"

"That response shows that you at least have some sensitivity."

"No, I was responding to the idea of spending another day cliff-hanging."

"You're going cliff-hanging?"

"Don't be dense."

"You don't like fooling around all day in suspense?"

"Welllll—"

"I knew it. You have the subtle look of a truly ravishing woman. You're planning on exhausting me again tomorrow! How *ever* will I get down to the shop on Monday?"

"Walk?"

"Who writes your material?"

Even pinned as she was in his bed, she did manage to shrug her shoulders. "You feed me the lines."

"I'll give up the shop, and we'll try Broadway."

She was doubtful. "The Broadway here in Fort Wayne?"

"We could make our start at the old Fire Station the Preservation Society saved. As hot as you are, you might need just such a place in which to perform."

With caution she inquired, "Perform?"

"You and that sassy tongue of yours."

"You like my tongue."

"Give me a very small kiss. I might be able to handle such a one."

She met him halfway, with neither of them having to move very much to do that.

He said in a grave tone, "Have I told you that this has been the greatest day in all my life?"

And her own voice wavered. "Mine, too."

But then he was silent. There were no further words, not of love or of commitment. He didn't ask if she had plans for the days ahead, nor did he make plans for things to do together.

Pat lay mostly under his lax body in his bed and was again convinced that their relationship was only a sometime thing. After all his years with Cheryl, he must value his freedom first.

She could understand that. She had felt as if she'd been released from a cage when Fred died. As fond as she'd been of him and as concerned as she'd been for his comfort and for his life, she had been freed by his death as Rod had been freed of Cheryl.

So, having such similar experiences in the caretaking of another person, why was it that, of the two of them, only she considered recommitting herself, while Rod could not?

Was it harder for the man? He'd really had no personal part in the care of Cheryl. He would have hired someone if Pat hadn't been just next door and volunteered to help.

Rod had accepted that Cheryl would be in his house and he had paid the bills. Even their doctor had come to the house to see Cheryl. Even he had known that to get the woman to an appointment was impossible.

But while Rod had paid out money and given consideration to Cheryl's comfort and contentment, he hadn't—ever—been trapped in a house with someone who seldom communicated.

Yes, he had.

She moved a little. Rod objected in a grouchy murmur. "Hold still. You're wiggling the bed."

"I have to go home."

"I spent the night with you last night—it's your turn to stay with me tonight."

She lectured with patience. "Your reputation is different from mine. I can't stay here without people gossiping."

"Let the tongues wag. Who cares?"

"I care."

"You're a big pain in—" His voice turned sly. "Would you like to know where you make me hurt?"

"I hesitate to inquire."

"Give me your hand."

"I'm not that rash. I need my hand."

"I'll give it back. This is like Show and Tell. This is called . . . Feel and Understand. It's for people in dark rooms."

"We could turn on a light and I could look?"

"Why, Patricia! You're an ogler? You seemed like such a nice woman."

"Well, yes. It's a facade I cultivate."

"You know how cultivating is done?"

"Of cou—"

"With plowing and planting." He shifted.

"Uh-uh-uh! Don't you dare."

"I was just going to show you how—"

"I really must be leaving. I have enjoyed the day. You're such a...different host. I don't believe I've ever even *heard* of anyone like you. I believe I shall look back on today and wonder how I ever managed."

He sighed elaborately. And his doing it that way made him think of all the times Felicia had been positive he had dramatic talent. He smiled. "You have a great deal to learn about men. Show me what little your husband taught you."

"You'll have to move off me."

"Oh. Sorry."

"You are nothing of the kind. You climb on top, deliberately, every time you get the chance."

"I thought I was more subtle than that. How did you figure that out?"

"I...was the...recipient."

"A vessel."

"Antonia Fraser wrote a book called *The Weaker Vessel*. The title referred to women and their being second-class citizens. Knowing that even four and five hundred years ago, they were trying to do something to help themselves. Do you realize women have been struggling for just a voice in their lives all through time?"

"I wasn't around until the last thirty-eight years."

"I've been seeing the difference for the last twenty-nine."

His voice doubtful, he enquired, "You started struggling for women's rights at...birth?"

"Just witnessing a birth, firsthand that way, one's attention is drawn to who gets all the fun and who does all the work."

"The baby?"

She drew in a large, very patient breath.

He said, "Your chest is just beautiful."

"I'm too little."

"Much more and you would be top-heavy."

"Are you trying to distract me?"

"We were talking about plowing and planting, and I was about to demonstrate how that was done when you slammed down your soapbox and started lecturing *me* about women's rights."

"It seemed like a good time to mention something along that line."

"Why?"

"I was saying, if you can recall, that I needed to go home because my reputation would be smudged if I spent the night in your house."

"Why?"

"It isn't done."

"Oh, yes, it is. And I stayed at your house last night."

"That's different."

"How?"

She took a couple of breaths to begin speaking a couple of times, then she said, "I'm not sure. But it is."

"I'll tie you to the bedstead and you can give that as your excuse, if anyone mentions that they know you stayed a night with me."

A night. Singular. This was to be her only opportunity to stay all night in his bed? Now, what was she to do? Was she a slave to her senses? Didn't she have any backbone at all? She replied, "Move. I must go home."

He grumbled, "What a stickler." But he...moved. "Last chance." He waited.

"It was a perfect day. Thank you."

"Stay."

"Structurally, I cannot."

"I'll walk you home."

He was giving up.

He shifted, and he kissed her a remarkably, gorgeously thrilling time, and her bones melted and her core heated and she moaned.

He lifted his head and his eyes glinted with his wicked pleasure that he'd made her react so, in her sated condition. He rolled off her, turned her over onto her stomach and swatted her backside very sassily.

"Go home and get some rest. You might need it." He lay back on his pillows and said, "I'll listen from here. If you need help, yell. There's the phone right here, and I'll dial 911 and get help to you right away."

She rose smoothly and looked down her nose at him. "You're a cretin." And she picked up her things and shook them out.

He folded his hands behind his head and looked thoughtfully at the dark ceiling. "A cretin? What *is* that? I've heard people called that—men mostly—and I've never known anything about what it is, except that it's an insult."

"A misshapen person with arrested mental development."

"Yeah, that about covers it." And he curled out of bed, his body hunched over, one long arm swinging as he lurched along toward her.

She squeaked and ran from his room, down the hall and to the back door.

He followed, loping along, making awful sounds. She got out the back door, still naked, clutching her clothes, and in the dark she ran across his driveway and over to her own house. She entered as the phone was ringing.

She picked it up and there were animal sounds. She said coolly, "You, again." And she hung up.

Eight

Inside her house, Pat had only closed the side door and walked to the stairs when Rod was at her door. She was still naked, her clothing in her hands.

He tapped on the door, calling, "Pat?"

"What is it?"

"What do you mean, what is *it?* 'It' is a Rod."

"Well, is something wrong?" She opened the door a portion and stood on the other side of the locked screen door.

"Unlock the door."

"I'm not dressed."

"I don't mind."

She opened the door wider, and her skin was faintly luminous in the dark.

He said, "I need shots to help me with my addiction to you."

"I don't know what the reverse serum would be."

"We should experiment."

Was he saying he wanted to be cured of needing her?

"Why are you here?"

"Why did you say, 'You, again,' when I growled at you over the phone?"

"I knew it was you."

"Oh. When you replied that way and hung up, I suddenly remembered reading that some people call other people and just make sounds. I thought somebody had been doing that to you."

"No."

"Open the door. I want to be inside."

"Go home."

"I have no home."

"It's right across your driveway."

Her voice was amused, but she didn't realize she'd used the label "home" for a house in which he had lived for some time. He explained, "It's just a house."

Her compassion at his revealing words made her hand unlatch the door, and he came inside.

"May I stay?"

"You should not."

"I know. Please."

How could she refuse? She not only loved him, she felt anguish for him. All the years he'd lived in that house, it had never become "home" for him. Think of his feeling of rootlessness, even as he had been honor-bound to his responsibility.

He kissed her. He ran his hands down her bare back and he kissed her. "I . . ." He stiffened. "I'm tired. Some woman has been at my body all this day long. Give me shelter."

"You're asking sanctuary?"

"Yeah."

"Come along."

She led him up the stairs, and he followed closely, his hands on her in odd places.

"Cut that out."

"I have night blindness. I need a seeing-eye woman."

She scoffed as she led him into another bedroom.

"Are you sleeping here tonight?"

"You are."

"Why just me?"

"So I can sleep."

"Oh."

He made no other comment or any objections. He took off his shorts and was gloriously naked. She looked on him with nonsalacious pleasure. Well, maybe a little.

She said, "You know where everything is."

He replied in a hushed voice, "Yeah."

She gave him sheets and pillowcases, then she went in to shower. She left the bathroom's night-light on and went into her room. She'd half expected him to be in her bed, but he was not.

Just a tad disappointed, she crawled into her bed and pulled the cover over her. She thought about Rod and how complicated he was and how afraid he was of any commitment, but she was too tired and she slept.

How long she slept she didn't know, but she was suddenly rigidly awake and opened her mouth to scream when a big hot hand covered her lower face and Rod said, "It's me."

She removed his hand and questioned with censure, "Why are you in my bed?"

"I get the night horrors. I'm afraid of the dark unless I have a brave woman close by for support."

"Go back to your own bed. I've been tussled around enough for one twenty-four-hour period."

"You have your period?"

"No."

"Is that good or bad?"

"Sssssssssshh!"

"PMS." His voice in the dark was satisfied with figuring the solution.

She made a throat-tearing sound of impatience.

"I'll rub your tummy."

"No."

The light went on and she flinched briefly before it was as quickly turned off. He whispered, "I was checking to see if you were the same woman who was in my bed just a short time ago over at my house."

"Good gravy."

He advised kindly, "Just settle down and sleep. Tomorrow is another day."

"You and Scarlett." Her words were disgusted.

"Will Scarlett? Wasn't he a highwayman?"

"Go—to—sleep!"

"Yeah."

She was excessively conscious that he was in her bed. His heat pulsated across the bed to her, warming her to the degree that she flung back the sheet.

He said, "Shh."

That really ticked her off. She took a couple of breaths to snarl at him, but she was just too tired to start anything and have to stay awake long enough to win. Slowly she relaxed, found she was matching his slow breaths, and she welcomed sleep. She drifted into deep sleep and slept heavily.

She roused as Rod sneakily laid her flat and very, very carefully parted her knees. She asked, "Just what are you doing?"

He whispered, "I have an anatomy test tomorrow and there're a couple of things not clear to me, so I thought since you're not doing anything else I could check them out. I'll just be a minute. Go back to sleep. I'll try not to jostle you."

And she laughed.

His rumble followed hers as he lay on her and slowly sank into her hot sheath and he sighed. "Ahhhhhh."

She didn't move a muscle.

She didn't have to. He writhed and gasped and pumped and went limp. He lay lax, his breaths slowing, and finally he pried himself from her carefully, kissed her cheek and left the bed.

She curled onto her side, just amazed by him. But she was almost asleep before he returned to the bed. She felt the bed dip and felt his careful movements in accommodating his body to hers. She felt his hot, quietened breaths. She again went to sleep, as she was thinking how different men could be.

She wakened alone in the bed. It was daytime. Feeling lazy and contented, she stretched and moved her body. She vaguely recalled really hot dreams. She looked at the other pillow. It was smooth. Had she dreamed Rod was there with her?

Had she dreamed that he came over saying he was afraid of the dark? And she doubted her memory. She'd been really tired last night. Yesterday had been a long and involved day. . . and she smiled at the ceiling. What a man.

She heard a sound downstairs. She frowned and listened intently. Pictures do fall off walls. They are always a surprise in the dead of night. Why did they never fall off their nails in the daylight hours when someone was in that room?

There was another sound.

She eased up in her bed, breathing shallowly, listening rigidly.

The stairs creaked. Someone was in the house? She opened the drawer by the bed and got out her gun. She lifted it. . . .

Rod walked in the door and dropped instantly to the floor in a clatter, yelling, "Hey!"

"Rod?"

"I've heard of women like you who want to deny everything the next morning. But shooting a guy is illegal."

"You scared me silly."

"I will not allow guns around the house."

"I'm sorry but you surprised me."

"You surprised me, too. My God, woman!"

He still lay on the floor amid the mess of the breakfast he was bringing up to her. She got out of bed and went to him. "You were bringing me breakfast."

"Yeah."

"You should. You were on me all night long."

"Only two or three times. Not enough for you to take a gun to me!"

She put his head on her bare thighs and took a napkin to wipe the egg out of his hair. "I could have hurt you."

"You could have *killed* me."

"No, I hadn't taken the safety off. I know how to handle a gun. You needn't have messed up breakfast that way."

With a good deal of irony, he replied, "I'm so glad."

"This is a mess."

"I'm just lucky that I'm not leaking a lot of blood."

She lectured, "I was only prepared to react, I don't shoot for no reason at all. I'm a woman alone. I have to take care of myself."

"We're getting rid of the gun."

"This is my house."

"Then we'll sleep at mine."

"I think you're overreacting."

"Have you ever carried breakfast upstairs to someone and been met by a gun in your face?"

"No. You're paranoid."

"I saw my whole life flash before my eyes."

"It was only a minu—"

"Fast-forwarded and it was all black space... nothing."

"You're very dramatic."

"Don't you ever tell that to Felicia."

"Your mother?"

"She nagged me all my life to be in her plays, and I never would. She said I had great stage potential, and if you dare to mention that you think I'm dramatic, I'll never hear the end of it. I am not. You just said that because you know you scared me spitless with that gun and you're trying to imply that I overreacted."

"We have a great civic theater here in Fort Wayne. They're doing—"

"Don't change the subject. I need calming and re-assuring."

She retrieved one of the strawberries, dipped it in some of the spilled cream and fed it to him.

He opened his mouth and accepted it while she smoothed his hair back from his face.

He suggested, "You're being kind so that I don't sue."

"Well, one does as one must. I doubt a jury would believe—for even a minute—that you're afraid of being alone in the dark and had to sleep over here and got into my bed for me to protect you from the things that go bump in the night. One look at the size of you and your credibility would be shot."

"Don't say that word."

He lay sprawled on the floor, his head on her bare thighs, her bare breasts just above him, her sweet face solemn and concerned. He was enjoying her attention, loving the way she teased him. He had known where the gun was the night before and he knew that the gun was on safety. He'd checked that, at the time, for his own information.

He allowed the different methods she used in soothing him. She put some of her thick jam on a bite of muffin. She was such an odd woman. So entertaining. What other woman would calm a man by feeding him from the debris of a meal splattered on the floor? Most women would be cleaning it up.

He accepted a slice of honeydew as he considered the fact he could never be sure where their conversations would go. Her mind worked ... differently. And it surprised him that he was learning to follow and explore...conversation. Who would ever believe that exchanging words could be an adventure?

How bleak his life had been. He'd thought it was only lacking in sex. Sex alone didn't make a relationship. There were more facets to share, to enjoy, to find.

Friends. Look at all the friends Pat had made who were fond of her. Those who welcomed her and therefore welcomed him.

How prettily she made her life. The garden, her friends, her home—for that is what she'd made of it—it was a home. The colors, the comfort, the things done to please the eye.

And he'd thought that, other than being celibate, he had been living a full life? No wonder Salty had said that Cheryl had crippled him. Rod hadn't understood Salty before then. His father's critical evaluation of how Rod's life had narrowed had only angered Rod.

But now he was beginning to understand how full a life could be. He looked up past Pat's sweet bare chest, to her serene face as she reached for another strawberry.

"Is your floor clean enough to eat off of it?"

"We'll see if you get sick."

See? Any other woman would have blustered or blushed, but Pat calmly said they'd see.

"I'm just glad you don't have any cats or dogs."

"Well, a cat would lick up that cream. And a dog wouldn't mind lapping up the scrambled eggs."

"You're weird, do you realize that?"

"Because cats and dogs like cream and scrambled eggs?"

"Because breakfast is all over the floor, and I'm lying here with my head on your naked thighs allowing you to feed me stuff that's scattered all over everything."

She lifted her eyebrows. "You haven't refused."

See? She didn't counter that he was the crazy one, she just mentioned that he hadn't objected to eating from the floor.

She continued to select available bits and feed them to him. And he ate them. Then she looked around and said, "Everything else is either too far away or too squashed."

But he lifted his head and licked the raspberry dot on her breast. She smiled down at him as he suckled. Her hands on his head supporting it, bending to make her nipple more available.

"How could you possibly be interested in sex at a time like this?"

He checked his watch. "Ten-eighteen? What's wrong with ten-eighteen?"

"I'm speaking of all the times last night—"

"You were asleep! You don't know anything about last night. You snored and swallowed and flopped around and never woke up!"

"Why? What was going on?"

"I've never met a woman who sets me off the way you do."

She scoffed.

"It's true. I've never been so sexual. Once a day would have been unusual. With you, I ache for you almost constantly. I want to touch you and feel your body and be inside you."

"So that's what you did last night?"

"I did let you get some sleep." He was serious, earnest as he assured her. "I didn't take you but a couple of times. Lying next to you was torture. I couldn't not take you."

"You could have gone back into the other room."

"That's too far away from you."

She didn't reply as she allowed his words to hang in the air. Was he listening to his words?

She leaned over and kissed his forehead, but he just caught her nipple in his mouth again.

She straightened, popping it from his lips, and he watched her with a small smile.

She decided, "I suppose you should shower. You're interestingly smeared."

"Lick me off."

She laughed as the temptation danced inside her.

He said, "If I let you bathe me, then you have to let me do you."

"That sounds fair. Come along."

He decided, "Me first."

He took up most of the shower. She had to slide around him and reach, and he countered by sliding his hands around her and reaching. She said, "Cut that out." She said, "Now, now, behave!" She said, "Ummmmm."

And she didn't get her shower for an intensely interrupted time.

They ate again on the porch. She had on that sinful kimono with a towel wrapped around her head. He had on the same old shorts.

"I think I ought to bring some of my clothes over here. This way, I'm limited to what I have on."

She indicated his house, on beyond her garden and his driveway. "It isn't far. You can go ho—to your house and change easily."

"What about this winter, when the icy winds are blowing down from Chicago?"

"You could be more careful with the clothes you have on."

Her words were fine. But she was thinking that he planned to continue this relationship through the winter? He was thirty-eight. He didn't speak of permanence, he spoke only of being together.

If he wanted the family he said he did, he ought to be looking for a wife. Because if she didn't suit him, after this intense relationship they were sharing, then he was wasting time with her. Was she simply a convenience? Was he just playing sexual catch-up after all the bleak years just past? When he got control of this surprise and avid interest in suddenly wakened sexual lust, would he then be finished with her?

Was he just using her willing, available body?

For her own sake, Pat knew that she should ease off with him. If she had any brain cells at all, she would. She shouldn't allow him to spend the night again. She couldn't bring herself to shun him as she should, but she needed to protect herself from his lure of companionship and delight.

He could ruin her for wanting any other man. She was only twenty-nine. She had a lot of years ahead of her, to use and enjoy and appreciate. She needed to behave and be careful of herself.

That was a good, logical lecture. She acknowledged that fact. She would pay attention.

He said, "I really like that kimono. Where did you get it?"

"In France."

"Let's go over there and buy you another. How would you like a weekend in Paris?"

She laughed.

"You have a nice laugh. It tickles around inside me."

"Surely not. Not again."

"Now, all I said was that I like the way you laugh."

"Then why am I on your lap instead of my chair?"

"Well, I'll be darned. How'd you do that?"

"Levitation?"

And again he laughed with her.

He said, "You're sassy and smug and withholding and a little too smart."

"What do I withhold?" She braced her hand on his bare stomach and stood up.

"Sex."

She whooped and gasped and put her hand to her head and was exaggeratedly careful in how she applied her bottom back to her chair.

"And you're selfish about it. You're not even using it and I could, but you make me wait—endlessly." He flung out one hand.

She sat straight, raised her eyebrows and just looked down him in a wonderfully studied disclaimer. "End—less?" She pinpointed that word.

He rubbed himself and said, "Well—" But he had to laugh. "What about Paris?"

"One is supposed to go to Paris in the spring."

"Next April? Maybe we can. Will that kimono last until spring?"

The kimono would—the real question was, would they?

He said, "I think I'll take tomorrow off. I haven't had any time off in so long that I find I'd like another day away from the shop. Do you play golf?"

"Ineptly."

"Great. We won't compete, then, and I'll look pretty good. It's been years since I played—" he looked at Pat "—anything." His face was sober and thoughtful.

"I have some appointments for tomorrow. I'm on call for a couple of single mothers. I'll have to see."

"How are you 'on call?' "

"We have a single mothers' program here for which volunteers are needed so that the mothers can make their classes. They take various studies in order to get better jobs. They are from either fatherless households or they are unwed mothers. Sometimes their sitters can't be there—our volunteers are on tap so the mothers can at least attend the classes."

"That's good. How are the kids?"

"About average. Nice, whiny on occasion. Quarrelsome at other times. And perfectly darling in-between."

"You're a pushover."

"No. I'm a disciplinarian. I go in and lay down the law and do everything their way."

"I can believe that. You ought to have some of your own."

"I might."

"You're not going with any guy."

What did he think he was? "No one who is serious." Him.

"I took up your weekend."

"I've enjoyed it. It had been a long time...since I'd been with a man."

"Why?"

"I hadn't wanted one." That wasn't true. She'd wanted Rod for how long?

"You mean...you're just sampling with me?"

How was she to reply? "Tasting the fruits."

"Well." He was thoughtful. "I'm glad it was me that was around when you decided you wanted some."

Could he be that stupid? She only looked at him.

"You're some woman."

She said nothing. Then her tongue said, "You're what any woman would desire."

His smile was slow as he watched her. And she blushed but she didn't lower her gaze.

"Let's go over to the fair at Kendallville."

"What sort of fair?"

"We'll find out."

Kendallville wasn't having a fair at that time. The town was a small one, quite charming, and people were either at lakes or snoozing in hammocks or visiting someone.

The lovers parked their car and walked up and down the main street to look in store windows. Then they went around the side streets to observe the fine houses and to admire the new library.

They went into an ice-cream store and bought cones and continued along, as they licked the ice cream and walked along contentedly. It was a charming town.

They had dinner back at Pat's. She had the dough, so she made the pizzas, and they were perfect. Rod had exactly what he wanted on his, and in what he thought were perfect portions. He became inventive and was very involved. He made cooking their dinner fun because of that.

They had lemon sherbet for dessert and sat on the screened porch in the candlelight, as the August day darkened down.

They told of things they'd done when they were children. And Rod told more about Salty and Felicia. He told what it had been like to be a part of such a strange expanded family. And he told how he'd hoped to have such a family himself. Then he sat in a pensive silence.

Pat told about her own young life. Her father had been an importer and she'd traveled a great deal. She'd gone to a boarding school and had enjoyed that enormously. It had been her first experience with living in one place for more than a couple of weeks.

After that, traveling on holidays had been a treat of a different sort. And she had enjoyed learning to buy and shop and seek. Her life had been one of marvel.

Her marriage had been quiet and stable.

Rod listened to those two words. He wondered if that had been what she'd wanted. "You could have been in the import-and-export business with your father."

"By then he was married to a Swiss lady, and mother was married to a Spaniard. I needed roots. I came back here."

"—and married Fred."

"Yes."

"And you were quiet and stable."

"I was in every organization in town. Name the organization and I've served on it until it was running steadily."

"You're an organizer."

"Was."

"So what do you do now, besides sit for women who go to school?"

"I work at the hospital, I paint scenery at the Civic Theater, I take classes at the art school out at IPFW."

"You fill your time."

"Because of illness, I had a husband who could have no social life. I needed to see other people."

"You're a fine woman."

"And I'm good in bed?"

"You are a man's dream."

So? What good was that? "You are a wonderful lover, Rod. I hope you realize that. I'm not very experienced, but there were several men. None for years, but I do remember. You are unusually considerate of the woman."

"Who were they?"

"Hmm?"

"The men . . . your 'several men.' "

She shrugged. "I'm not naming anyone. I only mentioned that because I wanted to compliment you."

"Would you be complimented if I'd said that I had a background of experience and therefore knew you were just great in bed?"

The hostility in his words was grating. His voice was roughened. He was offended because he didn't want to think of her with another man. Did he realize that meant he felt possessive? She looked at him and replied, "I'd probably not care for that."

He looked off into the dark beyond her lighted garden. He told her in a sour voice, "Neither do I."

"I beg your pardon."

"I didn't ask you to do that."

"I feel the need."

"Good God, Pat, leave it!"

She was silent.

It stretched. She sat still. He was restless in his chair. He stilled and then he said, in some shock, "We're having our first quarrel!"

She retorted sourly, "Hallelujah!"

"No. Don't be so snide. This is a milestone."

"How nice."

"You're really p—p—peeved with me. That's the beginning of friendship. Only true friends can get mad at each other and survive. Are we going to survive this quarrel?"

"On what terms?" There. She'd put it on the table. Let him state his intentions.

"That's easy. Don't you *ever* mention sleeping with another man to me."

"Oh, for Pete's sake."

"Well, listen here, Pat, talking about other lovers is taboo. Do you understand that? I mean it."

"So. All *right!*"

"Okay." And he smiled.

Nine

On Monday, they did play golf. They went in the slack morning hours where the grounds keepers weren't mowing. Rod was better than he'd mentioned and Pat didn't mind. Her game was rather carelessly mediocre.

They chose a cart and eased along, a few selected clubs in their bags. They encouraged being bypassed by other carts, and they relished the day.

They were not rushed and they allowed others to play through. They talked. They laughed. He sprayed her, placing his thumb on the water spigot at the drinking fountain, then he ran away from her revenge, through the sprinkler on the adjoining closed fairway.

They looked like drowned rats, but their eyes sparkled as they stood and laughed at each other until they were breathless. They never noticed that anyone saw them, nor the covetous male eyes that rested on Pat's soaked figure.

It was a throwback time for the pair. Neither had been carefree for years, not really. Their lives had taken a detour neither had anticipated, since lives happen in that way, and they'd lost years that should have been flavored with occasional balances of silliness.

Rod coaxed Pat to go into the rough, which had grown up and was concealing. There, he said, Pat could remove her coverings and dance the way the blonde had at "that awful place."

She declined. "I could disillusion some innocent cart boy in his impressionable youth."

"You'd inflame him to ravaging sexuality."

"If that's the case, it's just a good thing you were the aging male you are, when we went to 'that awful place,' and saw that blonde's enhanced body parts bounding around uncontrollably."

"You noticed that?"

"Who couldn't?"

"I never really saw her—"

Pat made a rather rude disbelieving sound.

"—because I was watching you. You didn't miss a wiggle. You watched as if that creature on the table were a specimen from a galaxy far away, who might never again appear in this one, and you might be called upon to describe or, worse, demonstrate just what she'd done here."

"Then you realize I'm basically an observer."

He could only laugh. He'd look at her, his eyes brimming with his laughter. He would try not to, but she'd look prissy and tolerant of him, and he'd be set off again.

They went to Hall's and collected a variety of foods and drinks and carried their picnic over to a grassy place on the bank of the river.

The golfers were territorial and paid for it, so they maintained their jurisdiction of the course. The kids still kept possession of the playground of colorful slides and swings and whirligigs. And the tennis players had those enclosed courts. The rest of the mowed grounds had been taken over by people who allowed their dogs to run free, but the grass wasn't yet as littered with droppings as Hyde Park by Queen's Gate in London.

Twice, big dogs challenged the picnickers' right to be in their paths. There was a man reading a newspaper in a car parked along the road, and Rod whistled shrilly to get his attention. The man looked up, Rod pointed at the dog and the man shook his head.

Finally, with one dog becoming hysterical, the pair moved into the pavilion and shared a table with two of the workers. Since Rod was with her, Pat felt free to exchange greetings and to ask questions. "Why aren't the dogs leashed?"

"They're supposed to be."

She asked with interest, "How do you like working for the park board?"

One worker looked around with elaborate interest. "Where's the mike?"

She replied, "I was just curious. I baby-sit."

"I could rent a kid."

Rod said, "I'm keeping her busy."

"Taking the day off?" one asked him.

Rod explained, "I'm unemployed."

So the other asked Rod, "How're you at driving a mower? Pay's lousy, but you get a good tan and skin cancer."

And when they left, Rod questioned Pat, "Do you always take up with strangers?"

She nodded gravely and confided, "I'm searching for the real Howard Hughes."

"There was a *purpose* in all those questions!"

"You couldn't for a minute believe that I'm an idle snoop."

"Uh—"

"I'm not."

When they arrived back at her house, the blinker on the telephone answering machine was on. Pat reached over and punched replay. Her mother had called from Spain to chat, but the next call was Alice's kids. "Mommy's hurt! Can you come over?"

Pat frowned at Rod and said, "Alice is one of the people I help on occasion. She has two kids, but no kin available at all. Her husband died riding tandem on a motorcycle and he wasn't wearing a helmet. No insurance. Stupid. Alice gets aid for dependent children and works to support them while she studies the computer at scheduled times. I'm a volunteer substitute sitter in the program to help single mothers in this initial training time. I have to call."

She did that. A woman answered the phone. It wasn't the usual sitter. She said, "It's serious. She slipped on a metal stair in the stairwell and it looks like she broke her neck."

Pat asked, "Can you stay there with the kids?"

"No. I have my own family. I've been waiting for you to call."

"I'll be right there."

Pat hung up and turned to Rod. "I'm sorry."

"First things first. How can I help?"

"I'll call you if there's anything."

"Give me the phone number and address. Call me and keep me informed about you."

She smiled, went to him and kissed him.

He hugged her very strongly and muttered in her ear, "Watch any stairs and walk carefully."

"Yes."

Pat showered and changed. Then she drove over to the Wilsons' house. It was small and needed work. Pat went inside, the sitter barely greeted Pat before she left. Pat had to follow the woman to the porch in order to thank her for staying with the kids.

The woman said, "I got my own to take care of."

Pat called the hospital and asked if the children could see their mother, Alice Wilson.

After Pat explained who she was and why she was calling and for whom, and under what circumstances, Pat was told the injury was worse than a broken neck. Alice was dead. Pat asked if the children could see their mother there at the hospital.

And they were welcomed. "Would you like their pastor to be here?"

"I don't believe they belong to any particular church, but if there is someone who has dealt with children in these circumstances, I would be grateful."

"Do you know the children well?"

"No. I'm a volunteer in the program for single mothers."

"You are the only one on her list of people to notify."

"She has only the children."

"Ahh. That's tough."

"Yes."

The boy was five and the little girl was not quite four. They were big eyed and worried.

They asked, "What about Mommy?"

"She was very, very badly hurt. Come, we'll go to see her."

There were people at the hospital who watched for them. Some already knew Pat because she did volunteer work there one day a week, pushing the book cart around to the rooms. And they knew that the mother of the children was dead.

The pastor was young. He was very kind. He said, "Have you told them?"

Pat shook her head.

He bit his lip and hesitated, then he asked the children their names. They looked at Pat. They'd been taught not to give their names to strangers.

Pat said, "I beg your pardon, I didn't introduce them. Pastor Jorkin, these are Alice's children. This is Sam and this is Mary. Children, this is the pastor here at the hospital. He is here to help people who are troubled and he would like to talk with you."

He said, "Come, let's sit down in here. We use this room especially to talk to God. He will listen to us anywhere, but this is a special place. I have sad news for you."

The kids crowded Pat. Their eyes were very serious and they pressed against the only known one there. Pat's emotions were fraying and she blinked tears.

With great gentleness and remarkable word choice, Pastor Jorkin told the children of their mother's death. He said the spirit leaves the body the way a butterfly leaves the cocoon. The cocoon was simply a temporary house the way the body holds the spirit. Their mother's spirit would go to heaven.

He told them very seriously, "She didn't want to leave you, but she was so badly hurt that her body died. She had no choice. You will feel her close to you now and then. What you feel will be her love for you."

With troubled eyes, Sam offered, "I saw a dead frog. It was squashed." Sam's eyes were tear filled and his face stubborn.

The pastor assured the boy, "Your mother wasn't squashed. She looks beautiful and peaceful. Come. We will go and see her. I will be with you."

Pat had liked Alice. Pat had known her in brief snatches for two years. She knew the kids better. She was suffering with them silently because she could not depend on her words to be as wise as those of the pastor.

He was so kind. He listened to the children and as their piping whispers questioned, the pastor explained with simple words.

Pat thought the pastor was remarkably calm until she noticed that tears reddened his own eyes.

They went down a hall to a quiet room to see Alice. She was lying on a bed and while her body was sheet covered, her hair was combed nicely, one of her arms was out from under the sheet and her hand was on her stomach.

The children questioned her, "Mommy?" And the pastor said that her hearing was gone from her body, just as her voice was no longer there. The children were not rushed at all. They touched her. "Mommy needs a blanket," Mary's little voice told them. "She's cold."

That almost undid Pat.

And the pastor told of the warmth of the spirit.

Both of the kids kissed their mother's cheek.

Pat told the pastor, "We would like to follow the hearse to the funeral home."

"Yes," he agreed. "We need to know which place. We have no instructions."

"Klaehn's is nearby. Would you call them to come? I will be responsible for this." She gave him her card.

"Why don't you go back to the chapel? This will take a little while."

"Could I use a phone? Not a public one."

"Come to my office."

Pat called Rod. "I need you."

"Where are you?"

And he was there.

He was so used to children. In the Brown home there had been so many who were all ages, and there had been those who had been through all the variety of problems. Rod knew what to do, and within minutes the children looked to Rod for answers and had one hand on him as their security in that strange, awful time.

Rod knew exactly how to handle that. He did it all so automatically. He touched their shoulders, their heads, and he said all the right things. And he didn't chatter.

Mary piped in a loud whisper, "Mommy's a butterfly."

Rod didn't allow it. "The pastor was giving you a parallel, an explanation, so that you can understand. Your Mommy's spirit is different from a pretty bug. You can't see her spirit. He meant that she can fly, now, like a butterfly."

"She's an angel?"

"I've never seen one," he assured the child, but his eyes looked up at Pat and rested on her in a benediction.

Mary asked, "Are you Pat's daddy?"

He replied, "I'm her love."

His face shimmered in her tears. But he hadn't said that she was his love.

To Pat, it had seemed important that the children know what happened to their mother. That she didn't vanish from the hospital and appear briefly at the funeral home.

That was done. They followed the hearse to the funeral home and then waited inside. Rod was completely supportive and explained things to the children in a matter-of-fact manner. They were allowed to see rooms in the funeral home and they were told enough.

They went back to their own house and would stay there that night. Pat stayed with them. It was too soon to move them to a strange place. Rod didn't like it that Pat was in that neighborhood.

"It's only poor, it isn't dangerous."

"I'll sleep on the porch."

"Don't do that. The mosquitoes are horrific."

"I'll be patrolling all night."

"If anything happens, Mrs. Simpson, across the street, will call the police. She's on social security, and she takes those words to heart. She sees to it that this neighborhood is socially secure."

He tightened his mouth and gave a patiently impatient sigh.

She almost smiled.

He helped her change the sheets on Alice's lumpy bed, and with the kids watching with big sad eyes, he didn't kiss Pat good-night. He patted her shoulder, touched each of the children's heads and finally left.

Pat fixed the kids some cereal, and they ended up sleeping with her in Alice's bed. Pat leaked tears all the night long in compassion for Alice, the mother who no longer would sleep there.

Alice was to be buried next to her husband in the cemetery. The children were familiar with the place, for they'd put flowers on their father's grave.

It was a tough three days. For the children it was very painful, so it was for Pat, too. And the childish questioning was exquisitely precise. They really didn't grasp exactly what was happening—or why—to their mother, and to them.

"What will happen to us?"

Pat wanted them to feel they had some say. "I could take you home with me until that can be decided. Would you rather stay here? Jeannie could still come during the day."

Sam decided, "We'll go with you."

Rod was indispensable. He helped them to move. He helped the children decide what to do with things they couldn't keep. They gave some things to their sitter, Jeannie.

Rod and Pat didn't entertain the children. They kept those days simple and quiet. They encouraged the kids to remember things about their mother. The children told of things they'd done together. Funny things and dear things were remembered.

They went to the funeral home several times in those couple of days. The adults were pressed to explain what was happening more minutely, with fewer words. When there were tears, they didn't chide the children for crying.

The funeral was rather well attended. The neighbors rallied around, Alice's co-workers were there and her computer instructor came.

Pat asked the mourners to explain to the children how they were known to their mother. It was touching how many people regretted Alice's death. Most deaths are regretted, it was just that lives were so busy that people hadn't the time to really notice for very long.

Once Rod said to Pat, "Cheryl had no real friend at her funeral, except for you. But she left no one regretting her death. That's very sad."

And Pat replied, "If friends were what she'd wanted, she would have had them. She had you, who allowed her to live as she preferred."

"Maybe that was the wrong thing to do."

"To have forced her into a routine or to be with acquaintances that would have annoyed her? What kindness would there have been in that?"

"Yeah. I see what you mean." And his last dregs of guilt left him. Cheryl had lived as she'd chosen.

And actually, so had Alice. They were two such contrasting people: Cheryl who was so sealed into herself, while Alice had been a striver. She'd kept her kids with her and was bettering her life because that was what she'd wanted. She'd been a good wife and mother, and she, too, had chosen her own way.

Rod said to Alice's children, "Your mother was a good woman, and you have every right to be very proud of her."

And *that* was the thing they could remember all the rest of their lives. Rod had said they had every right to be proud of their mother. And when they remembered his words as they grew older, they would understand why.

But in that time, as the children's lives were altered and changed, so was Rod's.

"No," said Pat. "You may not stay over. It would be confusing to the children."

And Rod was disgruntled. "I never got the rest of My Day."

"There could be another."

"How?"

"There must be a way," she assured him, but she made no effort to find one. She was busy with the children. She was oddly contented.

That was what irked the hell out of Rod, Pat was so... busy and contented.

They went swimming over at Abbots', but the kids went along. With permission and help from Merle, Pat invited other children the ages of Sam and Mary. They all had to be watched and helped and comforted and instructed. While Rod did that with goodwill and even enjoyed it, he eyed Pat's body inside that second skin, and he was restless.

But he listened to her laugh with the kids and he smiled as his ears soaked in those sounds. And the

Wilson kids began to laugh again. It had taken a while.

Pat saw to it that Sam's and Mary's acquaintance with other children expanded. She enquired about enrolling them in schools. And while she took them to place garden flowers on their parents' graves, she also took the children to other places. She had become very busy.

Once Rod said idly, "I think I'll adopt them."

"I've already applied."

He was shocked. "You didn't ask me."

"They're not your children."

"You *know* I was considering adoption."

"But you didn't even know these children. I did."

"You killed off their mother, waxing the metal stair?"

She took a deep, patient breath. "You are out in left field."

"Do you know what that means?"

"It's a baseball term, like 'play ball,' that people use as reference points."

"My God." He frowned at her.

"Now why are you calling God's attention to this conversation?"

"Because I'm irritated with you."

"Why?"

"Because I like the kids and want to adopt them."

"Sorry."

"You're really very independent. Why are you suddenly so maternal? Why didn't you and Fred have any kids?"

"Are you sure it's your business to know this?"

"Yes." The word was said emphatically.

"Fred couldn't have children."

"Why didn't you adopt, then?"

"He didn't want to cope with someone else's problems."

Obviously that was a direct quote, and Rod looked on Pat, knowing that she'd begged.

She was continuing. "Why didn't you?"

"Cheryl was incapable of supplying any care at all."

"You could have hired someone to care for the children. With some around, she might have come out of her shell."

He'd just gotten rid of the dregs of his guilt. "I asked. She could not give attention to another person. Had she, she would have had a meal ready when I got home from work. She would have changed her own sheets."

"Yes."

"So why didn't you adopt before now?"

"I am not long widowed, and I wasn't sure how my life would go." She suggested, "Go find your own kids to adopt."

"I hate for a woman to be in a position I can't alter."

But he could. He could join her in the adoption. He didn't mention doing that.

He asked, "How long does it take before the adoption is final? Why is it taking so long?"

"The lawyer has filed notice to see if there are any relatives and, if there are, if anyone would object to my adopting the kids. It's routine. I've never heard Alice speak of relatives. No one ever visited. He also says there's a chance of compensation being awarded to the kids for Alice's death."

As the days passed, the new family nucleus became more comfortable. The children's attention was widening beyond their grief. September was chilly. Sam was in preschool and took well to going. Pat found a nursery for Mary to attend three days a week. They were settling into a routine.

There, in Indiana, October's Indian summer would come in all its glory as the leaves turned and the brilliant colors of fall changed the trees. But to bring that change, the September temperature fluctuated. It could be forty degrees in the morning and close to eighty by afternoon.

Then Mary got an end-of-summer cold. How can kids adjust to fall? Pat had never been around sick kids. Not when she was the one responsible.

The nurse at the doctor's office was calm and soothing. "It is okay. It's a regular cold. If her temperature goes above 103 degrees, call us. Don't worry. The cough medicine and the children's aspirin should keep things under control."

But to Pat, Mary looked too pale and was too languid, and hearing Mary cough hurt in Pat's chest.

Rod came home from work and came first to Pat's house, as usual, and found a ragged Pat with anxious eyes. He asked, "What's wrong?"

"It's Mary. She's coughing so badly and she feels terrible. Should I take her over to Lutheran emergency?"

"Let's have a look." He headed for the stairs.

"She's in the living room. I can check her better if she's down here." Pat hovered behind Rod.

Surrounded by pillows and with three very clean dolls in various stages of wear, Mary was watching TV. She coughed and looked pitiful.

Rod said, "Hi, muffin." He kissed her forehead and took her hand. "She just needs a little knee and chest. The phlegm is clogging her a little."

Mary indicated the TV and said, "I'm watching."

Rod replied, "Okay. When there's a commercial."

"Knee and chest?" Pat inquired.

"You either actually put them in that position or tilt them that way over a stack of pillows. Then you pat their backs from the waist to their shoulders and it loosens the phlegm. They breathe easier."

"You've done this."

"I've told you how many hundreds of kids lived with—"

"Hundreds?" Pat was patently disbelieving.

He gestured. "It seemed that way. Kids get sick on occasion. Mostly, it's no big deal."

"How like a male to say something idiotic like that."

"No, I had to help, along with all the other kids. We were taught everything we had to learn in order to have a family and take care of people."

As he had taken care of Cheryl. But had he? Pat had. He'd allowed it. In his experience, sick people got well. But Cheryl hadn't changed.

With a car commercial, Mary allowed them to up-end her into the knee-and-chest position, and Rod demonstrated and patted. Mary coughed hard, and Pat fretted.

He explained, "The purpose is getting rid of it. This will help."

Pat frowned and watched with some stubbornness.

After fifteen minutes of patting, while Mary watched the TV sideways, Rod sat her back up and told her to drink ten swallows of the lemonade. She did. She was so interested in what was on TV that she was quiet. No gurgling, no rasping, she breathed clear.

Rod said, "Simple cold."

"How would you like to be resident nurse?"

"I get to move in?"

"They work eight hours a day."

"—from five to one in the morning?"

"Or a split shift?"

"How much?"

"Home-cooked meals?"

"No side dishes?"

She smiled a cat's smile.

He guessed, "You've missed me a little?"

"Come into the kitchen."

He didn't hesitate.

She turned against him and he kissed her witless. Her feet shuffled and she pulled back enough to say, "Sh-h-h!"

He growled, "That was you scrabbling to get closer."

"I'm not that type."

"Hah!"

Sam came into the house, sweaty and busy. He'd been playing next door with two other boys. He said, "Hi, Rod," and went to the sink to stand up on a new step-up so that he could easily get a glass of water. "It smells good." He turned to smile at Pat.

She said sassily to Rod, "He believes I'm a superior cook."

"Peanut-butter sandwiches, again?"
She put her hand to her head.
With Rod there, all was well.

Ten

Rod was still hesitant in committing himself to Pat. He could take the kids, he could help out with them, he could be available for counsel, he could want Pat to share his life, but he just couldn't quite bring himself to get entangled in another marriage.

Pat would hire a sitter for the children, so that she could go out with Rod, and they would laugh and share and they would make love. They made greedy, passionate love. Their bodies were hungry for each other, and their tussles were a little wild from their hunger having been held back. It was always that way the first time.

Pat assumed that it would never be any different. Rod had had every opportunity to indicate that he wanted her permanently. He showed that he cared about her, he relished their time together, he obviously enjoyed sex with her, but he never made any plans for the future. Not with her.

She lectured herself in the mirror. She argued and gestured and bit her lip and frowned and sighed and was impatient. But she finally acknowledged the relationship that they shared would be all that she would ever have with him.

The great problem was that she understood. How can a woman rant and rave and rend her clothing over something she understands?

He had entered his marriage with Cheryl with the long view of sharing and it hadn't worked at all. He was hesitant at age thirty-eight to recommit himself.

She needed to organize her life so that she wasn't waiting for his attention. She told Rod that. "I'm interested in marriage."

He went still and waited.

She said nothing else, and after a pause she went on to another subject. She felt she had given Rod all the push a man needed. He could have replied in various ways. Instead he'd remained silent.

She dated another man.

Rod was furious! He waited for her to be delivered back to her house. In the dark, he stood in his driveway with his hands on his hips and waited for the guy to leave. The man kissed Pat!

Rod saw red.

His head swung like a bull's as the man walked back to his car, got in and drove away. He had given Rod a blank, curious glance, but he hadn't paused.

As the stranger's car disappeared, Rod strode over and rattled Pat's door with his fist.

She came, after what seemed a long pause, and she said, "Well, hello, Rod," as if they were casual acquaintances and need not consult with one another or explain their conduct to one another.

"Who was that clown?"

"What clown?" Pat then leaned forward and looked around the yard with some interest, moving her body and turning her head to catch a glimpse of the clown.

"The guy who just kissed you?"

"He isn't a clown."

"What are you doing, running around with another man?"

"I need to widen my acquaintance. I'm almost thirty, I have two children, I would like a husband."

"So you're going around sampling and seeing if anyone suits you."

"Well, I haven't jumped into bed with anyone but you. You can hardly accuse me of . . . sampling."

"We live next door and we get along okay. You don't need to look around."

"I need commitment."

"I'm committed. I haven't dated any other woman."

"That's lazy. I'm handy. You like it this way. It isn't enough for me."

"You like me. You like making love with me."

"That is true. But I want more. I need commitment. You aren't willing."

He hesitated, agitated, at least for a man like Rod. He could find no words. "Well—"

"I'm not trying to force you. I have waited. You really aren't ready. I need to find someone who is."

"I've given you all my time."

"That's true. This summer will stay as a memory that I'll take out and look at in years to come. It's been so special."

"But not special enough. You don't care for me...enough."

"That isn't the problem, Rod. The problem is that you don't consider me as a love. You've labeled me as 'a widow bearing casseroles,' something to avoid, as a 'situation,' a 'premise' and a 'mechanism.' I've never been your love."

"Words are empty. I've heard people who hated each other say 'honey' and 'dear,' and they didn't mean anything by the terms."

"As I've told you, I do understand. I am not the one chiding. You are. You want a playmate. I want more."

"Well, I..." But he could not say the words. They stuck.

"It's late. Good night, Rod."

"Yeah." But the word was bitter.

"We had such a wonderful summer. I've never played or laughed so much in all my life."

"You could have warned me."

"About what?"

"That you weren't really interested in me."

"I don't know what else I could have done. I gave you the freedom of me. You're the one who kept me from moving away from the temptation of you."

"I was why you were leaving?"

"Yes. You must know that. You must have known. I thought you were interested in Glenna."

"But you know—"

"Yes. You told me."

"Why did you stay?"

"How could you not know that?"

"Do you love me?" He watched her with a scowl.

She looked at him for a long time. Her face was serious. "I allowed you to make love with me."

"That's a common trap."

"I didn't know that."

"Then you love me?"

She took a deep breath. "Yes."

"Why didn't you want to tell me that?"

"I was afraid that you would feel you had to do something about me. I wanted you to love me free and clear."

He put his head in his hands and groaned in anguish. "Oh, Pat."

Although he obviously suffered, he was silent.

Softly, softly, Pat said, "Good night, Rod."

When he didn't reply, she stepped back, gently closed the door and shut the inside door.

Rod stood outside for some time. She knew that, because she waited to see if he would tap on her door to talk with her. He did not.

Two days later, Pat's lawyer came to her house. She was surprised to see him there midday and said so. "Well, hello! What are you doing here?"

Drew Thompson took a deep breath, then a couple more, and declined to be seated. He paced with slowness and looked around as if only interested. A good man, his agitation was well controlled. Had it not been midday, Pat wouldn't have thought he was restless, but she was alerted.

"Pat."

She waited.

"Pat. I have some good news and some bad news. I find it hard to tell you."

"I'm broke?"

"No. You know the state of your fortune. It's the kids. They have relatives. A lawyer over in Iowa contacted me. By the greatest chance, they saw our notice. Alice's husband had a raft of relatives over in Pella."

"Oh."

"Yes."

Pat's face was without expression.

"Ross Wilson had his parents, sisters and a brother, uncles and aunts and grandparents. There are nieces and nephews the children's ages. There are cousins to the fourth degree. They thought they'd lost touch forever with Ross. They hadn't known he was married. They grieve for his death, they are stunned because they never knew about Alice, but..."

Drew didn't seem to be able to say it, so Pat supplied the words. "They want the kids."

"Yeah."

There was a long, long silence. And Drew was perfectly still.

Pat took an unsteady breath. "I believe I need to cry."

"I have two handkerchiefs and I can hold you."

She looked up at him and saw that his own eyes brimmed. Why did there have to be so many tears in this world?

And Rod came over.

It was mid-afternoon. He wasn't due home. But he was there. How strange.

He called, "Pat?"

"Yes."

"What's going on?"

"How did you know?"

"Do you mean to tell me something is?" Rod opened the door and came inside without an invitation. His hostile gaze lighted on Drew and he said in a softened snarl, "Who are you?"

And Drew turned to Pat. "Do you want him in on this?"

"What!" Rod advanced a little stiff-legged.

"Rod. Wait. Drew is my lawyer. Some Wilsons have contacted him. The children have a good many relatives over in Pella, Iowa. They want the children."

"My God."

There was a silence, and they faced the bleak fact that the children should go to Iowa.

Pat asked, "How is this done?"

"We talked about it," Drew told her. "The children have been through so much. But if they must change, they shouldn't get too entrenched here. We can still be careful. Some of the Wilsons will come over and start getting acquainted. The grandparents and a couple of great-grandparents and a few little cousins at first?"

Pat's voice was lifeless. "Oh. Yes. That's probably how it should be."

"Their lawyer, a Mr. Botherly, said the family felt great compassion for you. I've told them about you. That you are very kind to the kids."

"Yes." Pat answered absently.

Rod said in an emotion-roughened voice, "Thank you for coming out and telling her personally. Could we contact you later? This has boggled Pat."

Drew asked Pat, "Are you all right? Would you like me to come back in a day or so?"

"Yes."

Rod elaborated that. "We'll be in touch."

"Pat, I am sorry about this." Drew took her hands.

"Thank you for coming."

Drew instructed, with compassion, "Call me tomorrow and let me know if I can help in any way."

"I'll need their names, and how to—"

Drew explained, "I meant that if you need anyone to help you through this, to talk or to be with someone, call me. I can come anytime."

That made Rod hostile.

But Pat put her hand on Drew's arm and Drew covered her hand with his own. She said, "Thank you."

Drew ignored Rod and pressed, "Do you want me to stay now?"

"Thank you, no. I need to think how to do this, after I'm able to accept that it must be done. I need to do that first."

Drew shook his head sadly. "It would be futile to fight it."

"I know." She sighed tiredly.

Drew began, "Pat—"

Rod said, "I'll see you to the door." And he crowded Drew with some practice. He'd grown up with occasionally recalcitrant kids.

Drew wasn't very crowdable. He gave Rod a tellingly threatening glance and asked Pat, "Do you want me to clear you of...company?"

"No, thank you. Leave Rod alone."

"All right." But Drew looked hard at Rod and his stare was not kind. "You behave," he growled under his breath.

And Rod retorted, "She's mine."

Drew continued to look at Rod and he took his own sweet time leaving Pat's house. Rod didn't hustle Drew at all, but every inch Drew relinquished, Rod accepted and held.

With just Rod and Pat to hear Drew's car leaving down the street, they then heard the empty silence. That was especially poignant to Pat. She had once accepted silence as a part of her life, but she'd recently acquired the means to fill that silence in her life, and her soul groaned that she would have to give up those two busy, noisy little children.

They were to move away across two states and they weren't old enough to remember much about this time of being a part of another woman's life. How could she let them go?

Rod didn't even ask. He gently lifted her into his arms and went out onto the screened porch that was warm in the late October sunshine. He sat on a rocking chair and rocked Pat silently.

They were quiet for a long, long time. He said, "You can't grieve when they have a big family who wants them."

"I know."

"I've never known who my people were. I'm a real orphan. I don't know any genetic information or what they looked like or anything. It's just as if I were hatched from an egg left in the middle of nowhere.''

"You suit me.''

"You have me.''

"Yes. Thank you for coming. How did you know to come to me?''

"Damned if I know. I was busy, but I told Twila, 'Pat needs me,' and I just came. I must love you a whole lot to do that.''

"Yes.''

"You have me. I'm yours.'' He said that very seriously.

"Thank you.''

"You're welcome. You have to be careful of me.''

"I will.''

"And I'll see to it that you have the best care I can give a woman.''

The words shivered Pat. Cheryl had emptily occupied all those years. "I'm perfectly capable of caring for myself.''

"I'll see to it that you are, so that you can take care of me.''

"Are you going into a decline?''

He nodded once very seriously. "Ever since you said you were looking for a husband. When I came in here and found that yahoo here, I thought he was why I was supposed to get over here and stop him. I thought I was going to have to throw him out of here and stake my claim.''

"Are you declaring for me?''

"You can't be that dense. Why else would I be here and holding you on my lap this way?''

"I don't know.''

"I . . . want you to marry me."

"You can do better than that."

"You are the pickiest woman I've ever met. You want me down on my knees?"

"I'll see. I'm still a little distracted. I really love those kids."

"We'll get a bunch."

"How?"

"I'll ask my dad. He collects stray kids."

"Not…right away. I have to have time to adjust to losing Sam and Mary. They are such sweet children."

"Around you, any kids would be darling."

"You're prejudiced."

"Yeah."

"Are you asking me to marry you because you're sorry for me?"

"No. I would've gotten to it. I couldn't stand to see you kiss another man."

"So you were jealous?"

"Very possibly."

"I was jealous of Glenna."

"She was really tempting, all the way up until she called me 'Sidney.' That poor guy."

"I can't help but be glad she blundered."

"Why."

"Because I've loved you for a long, long time."

"You never said a word."

"How could I have done that?"

"Aren't you curious why I tried for Glenna?"

"I believe I can figure that out by myself."

"I really wanted you. I'd found I was always conscious of you. I tried not to be at the house when you were there. I thought it was just because you were perfect and in such a contrast to Cheryl. But it was you. I couldn't take another woman. Not even wiggly Cindy."

"Just what did she do that day you came back from visiting your folks?"

"She was a temptation."

"Yes?"

"Yeah."

"You don't intend telling me, do you?"

"You're too young."

"It's going to be very, very hard to give up the children, Rod. I can't bear to think of it."

"In those circumstances, you concentrate on *them*. You know it's right for them. You know you could make them feel awful, leaving you, so you help them. You make it easy for them and in doing that you ease yourself."

"You're a very fine man."

"No. I am hurting for you, and if you are hurt badly I'll suffer with you, so I'm trying to figure a way for you to be calm so that I can get through this separation and the kids can go free without wrecking me."

"Then this is all selfish?"

"That's about it."

"This is probably proof that love is blind. I still love you."

"Thank God for that."

He kissed her then. He kissed her sweetly, and though he sweat and trembled, he made no move to make love to her.

Of all the things he'd told her, that restraint convinced Pat that Rod did love her. And it was a good love.

Preparing the kids for their change in living and in moving was carefully done. It took visits, back and forth. The Wilsons welcomed Pat and Rod to Pella so that the pair could check them out and see how and where the children would be with an uncle and aunt. They saw the rooms the kids would have, and the places they'd go to school and the neighbors they'd know.

Everyone was very kind. How could Pat grieve for children whose lives would be fitted into a perfect slot? Perfect, that is, given those circumstances.

It was arranged that the bodies of Alice and Ross would be moved to the Wilson cemetery plot in Pella, and that was done.

All of the Wilson family branches met at the home of the grandparents who lived on a farm. The kids got to watch the cows being milked and they got to climb up into a loft. They were absorbed by cousins and they laughed until their cheeks were pink and their eyes dancing.

A Wilson who was middle-aged asked, "How will we ever thank you for helping Alice? What was she like?"

And Pat could tell them. She didn't tell them of the compensation. She would let Drew do that through the other lawyer after the move was settled. She didn't want money to influence any decisions.

But as Pat became acquainted with the Wilsons, she doubted knowledge of that money would have made any difference.

As they drove back to Indiana, Pat told Rod, "Those two kids landed on their feet."

"You already had them there. They were secure all along the way. They knew they were loved and that someone would care for them. Alice, and then you. They've been luckier than a lot of kids who have both parents."

"Life can be very strange."

"If my life had been different," he told her somberly, "I would never have known you."

"I lived next door."

"I meant in the Biblical sense."

"Ahh."

"I wasn't being salacious. I was being awed."

"Do I awe you?"

"You scare the hell out of me."

"Now why would you say that?"

"I could lose you. Nothing's guaranteed."

"Don't be afraid for me. You could spoil the time we have. We'll think long. Years and years and years."

Pat and Rod called her parents who lived in Switzerland and Spain. They were interesting, busy people who were delighted their only child was to be married again. They did show some curiosity about the man she'd chosen as her next husband.

They were courteous and invited the pair to visit when it would be convenient.

"When will you marry?" inquired Pat's mother with polite interest.

"We thought maybe later this year. Would you like to come to our ceremony?"

"Oh, yes. I believe we'll be free."

While her response had surprised Rod, Pat appeared to accept such a casual interest as normal.

Rod mentioned, "I need to take you home to meet my parents and all the various siblings that can be gathered. You're in for a treat."

Pat wasn't at all tremulous about meeting Rod's family. She was secure enough in his regard that she didn't believe anyone could influence him contrarily.

It was November and Thanksgiving when the lovers arrived at the Brown house in Temple, Ohio. They drove up to a rather impressive collection of vehicles, all parked around a side yard, under a great big old elm that had survived the Dutch elm disease of twenty some odd years before.

Rod mentioned, "The house is painted. I helped last spring."

Not knowing about Abner's long, drawn-out delay, Pat said courteously, "It looks very nice."

Salty and some of the men and most of the kids came out, yelling and ragging and hooting to their eldest brother. And they smiled at Pat, not sure how not to scare her away, there were so many of them.

Salty kissed her forehead and said, "I'm glad you're here with Rod."

And Rod said, "She's one of the widows."

Salty rasped, "You're a lucky man. You should only beware of the scary ones."

In the noise and shifting of all the people inside that big old house, Pat met everyone.

Jo, who was the eldest natural son's wife and rather large with that son's child, said, "Bob's room is ready for Rod and you get Mike's room next door. And don't worry about instantly knowing all the names. We all know yours. Tell us what you might need."

And Pat said carefully, "Aren't you and Bob living in the attic?"

Jo laughed and said, "So you've heard about that?"

"Rod wondered how to get you out of it so we could have it."

"You might feel better knowing, now, that there's a connecting door between your rooms. Don't complain about two rooms, you two are the only ones sleeping solo. Or... at least, you can start out that way."

And Pat met Felicia. In her marvelously humorous and clever voice, Felicia told Pat, "It was Rod who convinced me I should marry Salty. He was such a darling boy. He still is, of course, as you must well know. He is an original. I did try to get him onstage, but he stubbornly refused. He said he had no drama to him."

Pat tattled, "Felicia, you were right. He is magnificently dramatic."

"Oh, darling, how I would love to know how you found that out!" Felicia laughed that wonderful way of a woman sharing with another the foibles of dear men.

In the maelstrom of people during that holiday, Pat met each and every single person. She would consult the mental chart she'd contrived and sort them out, mostly right.

At one time, as they spoke with Salty, Rod mentioned, "She believes I'm a Martian."

Salty looked at his eldest and said, "That's what it was. I always knew there was something, some clue I was missing. You've hit it exactly, Pat."

All in all, being absorbed by the Browns, en masse, was an experience. And in the night, as Rod came in and slipped into her bed, she would chide him, "We are guests here."

"I already knew that you are. I'm family. You have to work your tail off to convince me that you want to become a Brown."

"Oh? And how do I do that?"

So he sighed and again showed her how that was done. She exclaimed and commented in whispers and allowed that the instructions were very clear, after one understood his wording. Exactly.

Rod held her closely to him and he told her, "You're mine."

Her parents in amazed attendance, Pat and Rod were married at the Brown house at Christmas. It seemed appropriate. Rod was the eldest of the adopted children, and Bob was the eldest of the birth children. Bob and Jo had been married on Christmas Eve the year before.

Bob and Jo said, "The reception is so terrific as a party and everyone has so much fun that you won't want to leave. Since we stayed, we got the attic for our honeymoon. Stay and we'll give you the attic for that one night."

It was a great party. They laughed and teased and had such fun. And so did her parents and their spouses who had attended. The Browns knew how to give parties.

And after their night in the attic the newlyweds parted from all the mass of people rather late the next morning and went home to Fort Wayne.

They had decided to use Pat's house. And that night Pat showed Rod how she could dance on a low coffee table, naked and as well as any wiggling female who was attracting a man. He was scandalized and delighted. He whooshed out air and coughed and laughed.

He was delighted by her, besides being charmed. That she would taunt and tease him in that manner was thrilling to him. And he carried her up the stairs and made delicious love to her willing body. To her mind. To her soul. He really loved her.

It was only about two months after that when Salty called and said there were two little boys who needed a home. Would Pat and Rod help out?

"Boys?" Pat asked.

"Yes. I'm a boy," Rod mentioned. "You don't mind boys, do you?"

"Oh, no. But I'd want a little girl, too. Or maybe several."

"Honey, give me a chance. I've only been practicing. I'll get serious."

"All right."

And they did. They never did have as many kids as Salty and Felicia, but they had a good share. And they lived Rod's Happily Ever After.

*   *   *   *   *

SILHOUETTE® _Desire_™

Beginning in August
From
Silhouette Desire
Lass Small's
Fabulous Brown Brothers

When the Brown Brothers are good, they're very, very good.
But when they're bad . . . they are fabulous!

Read about Creighton, Mike and Rod in Lass Small's upcoming
Fabulous Brown Brothers series. And see if you don't agree.

In August—A RESTLESS MAN (SD #731)
In October—TWO HALVES (SD #743)
In December—BEWARE OF WIDOWS (SD #755)

Boys will be boys . . . and these men are no exception!

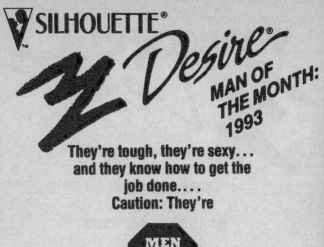

What a year for romance!

Silhouette has five fabulous romance collections coming your way in 1993. Written by popular Silhouette authors, each story is a sensuous tale of love and life—as only Silhouette can give you!

SPRING FANCY
Three bachelors are footloose and fancy-free... until now.
(March)

Mother with Love
Heartwarming stories that celebrate the joy of motherhood.
(May)

SILHOUETTE SUMMER Sizzlers
Put some sizzle into your summer reading with three of Silhouette's hottest authors.
(June)

SILHOUETTE Shadows
Take a walk on the dark side of love—with tales just perfect for those misty autumn nights.
(October)

Silhouette CHRISTMAS Stories
Share in the joy of yuletide romance with four award-winning Silhouette authors.
(November)

Silhouette®
A romance for all seasons—it's always time for romance with Silhouette!

PROM93

In the spirit of Christmas, Silhouette invites
you to share the joy of the holiday season.

Experience the beauty of Yuletide romance with Silhouette
Christmas Stories 1992—a collection of heartwarming stories by
favorite Silhouette authors.

JONI'S MAGIC by Mary Lynn Baxter
HEARTS OF HOPE by Sondra Stanford
THE NIGHT SANTA CLAUS RETURNED by Marie Ferrarella
BASKET OF LOVE by Jeanne Stephens

This Christmas you can also receive a FREE keepsake Christmas
ornament. Look for details in all November and December
Silhouette books.

Also available this year are three popular early editions of
Silhouette Christmas Stories—1986, 1987 and 1988. Look for these
and you'll be well on your way to a complete collection of the
best in holiday romance.

Share in the celebration—with Silhouette's
Christmas gift of love.